CW01650565

HER SISTER'S KILLER

An absolutely gripping killer thriller full of twists

MICHELLE S. SMITH

JOFFE BOOKS

Joffe Books, London
www.joffebooks.com

First published in Great Britain in 2021

Cover art by Nick Castle

ISBN: 978-1-78931-892-0

CHAPTER 1

On the point of leaving her Morgan Park apartment, Victoria Wharton took a breath and glanced back at her reflection in the bedroom mirror one last time. The stiff work jacket that she always wore had been tossed onto the floor in a crumpled heap, along with her familiar tailored trousers. Just for tonight, she promised herself, she would forget that she was Detective Wharton. Tonight, she was just Vicky.

She had selected, from the back of her closet, a claret-red cocktail dress, spaghetti-strapped and falling just below her knees. It had been years since she had worn it, she realized. Victoria spun around, causing the gentle folds of the fabric to flare out. Her earrings, silver hoops, caught the light as she twirled. For a moment, she considered tying her hair back, but it had felt so liberating tugging loose the bun she wore for work. Instead, she simply brushed her hair away from her face so that the dark curls didn't obscure her earrings. She leaned closer to the mirror to check her make-up, hardly recognizing herself with darkened lashes and blood-red lips. Impulsively, she pulled open her bedside drawer and slipped on a silver bracelet, a gift from her twin sister.

She smiled back at herself as she turned to leave, and the young woman reflected in the glass smiled in return, looking coquettishly over her shoulder. Enticed by the thrill of the Chicago night air, which beckoned her with its promise of bright lights and the intoxicating excitement of chattering and laughter, she felt drawn to the unknown world beyond the safety of her four walls. *I am ready*, Victoria said to herself. Ready to go out. Ready to be admired. Ready, finally, to risk meeting someone. *Maybe even tonight*, she thought, her pulse quickening.

Picking up the photo frame from her bedside, the only one in her home, she repeated the words to the young auburn woman in the picture. "I am ready," she told her twin. Rebecca, slightly shorter and more fragile in appearance than her sister, was smiling, as she usually was. Her violet eyes, unlike Victoria's, held no skepticism. They gazed out uncritically at the world. Of its darker undercurrents — the jealousies, manipulations, violence, betrayal and greed that Victoria witnessed every day — she seemed oblivious.

Victoria's attention was distracted by her phone vibrating in her bag. She glanced at the caller ID, and sank onto her bed, staring at the screen. The phone buzzed impatiently. She hovered her finger over the 'cancel' icon. *Not now.* But she couldn't do it. She took a breath and accepted the call.

"Mother."

How long had it been since she had left her mother and her past behind in New Hampshire?

"You should never have left Hancock." She had heard it all before, but something in the uneven breathing was new, and it unsettled her. Her mother's voice held a dryness as brittle as fallen leaves. "Something terrible has—" The silence that followed these words was worse than the fragmented breathing.

"What's wrong?"

"Your sister didn't arrive at the hospital for work and they—"

"Becky's missing?"

Victoria's question hung between them. The silence seemed to last forever.

“Her body was found this morning by a jogger. They’ve just let me know.”

“Her body?” Victoria repeated blankly. “Was — was it an accident? A seizure?”

The voice on the other end faded till it was little more than a whisper.

“Murder.”

CHAPTER 2

Victoria sat dully on the wooden floorboards of her apartment, her packed cases stacked around her as she waited for first light to leave for Hancock. She had managed to snatch an hour's sleep in between throwing whatever she thought she might need into bags, but her dreams had been nightmares, filled with the monsters she thought she had finally conquered, and she'd woken up with her pillow wet, though whether from tears or sweat she wasn't sure.

She hugged the photograph of her sister close to her chest and rocked slowly back and forth, too exhausted to think properly. Becky had always been the one with the bigger dreams — and the softer heart. It was probably her gentleness that had, in the end, destroyed any chance of her achieving her own goals. Victoria shut her eyes, trying to push away the memories that were hurtling toward her through the darkness, but they kept coming. Piercing through them, her mother's reedy voice, monotonous and complaining, threw accusations at her. Unwillingly, Victoria's mind zoomed in on the day she had walked away from it all.

* * *

"And now you are going to leave me too," her mother, Vera, said flatly. She turned her wheelchair away from Victoria, leaving only a side view of her back, twisted by scoliosis. She stared out into the garden through the peeling window frame, once immaculate white. When the girls were little, roses had filled the beds and a neat hedge running the length of the garden border had been regularly clipped and shaped. Now, the hedge was overgrown, and only a motley collection of roses remained. "You are just like your father was."

She shifted her wheelchair slightly as she said this, and her eyes slid shrewdly up to Victoria's face. At the mention of him, Victoria's hand had risen subconsciously to her throat. She massaged the constricting muscles until they relaxed.

Rebecca, so different in looks to her sister but so close in understanding, quickly intervened, dropping to kneel beside her mother's wheelchair, her willowy figure graceful. She had always moved with the fluidity of a dancer.

"Vicky is nothing like Dad was," she said calmly. "She is just pursuing the career she loves."

Vera stroked Rebecca's hand, her eyes filling with easy tears.

"You are such a sweet girl," Vera murmured. "I know you would never leave me, would you? I would die if you did."

Victoria glanced at Rebecca, waiting for her to tell their mother she was going away too.

"I've always relied on you, Becky," Vera continued. "Such a source of support." Her fingers closed over Rebecca's hand, gripping it with frightening strength. "My source of support," she repeated, watching her daughter's face closely. "It is knowing you are nearby that keeps me going—"

"Tell her about Stanford, Becky," Victoria interrupted.

"I haven't decided yet," Rebecca said, dismayed to see the tears tumbling onto her mother's hands.

"Yes, you have," Victoria insisted. "No one who has been accepted to study medicine at Stanford turns it down.

You have dreamed of being an oncologist for years. Don't let her do this to you."

Vera drew in her breath.

"Are you suggesting I would try to sabotage my daughter's happiness?" she said slowly, lifting her head to stare at Victoria. "Is this all the thanks I get for everything I have given up for you? All my money, gone with the divorce, my health, destroyed by the stress—" Her voice cracked. "Your father. He would never have left if it weren't for you and your — *insinuations*. Would he?"

The words seemed trapped in Victoria's head, echoing inside her mind until she felt dizzy and nauseous. Her mother's image danced in a hazy mirage before her eyes. She wanted to shout, but her mouth and her brain wouldn't work together.

"I'm leaving," she heard herself say.

"Go then," her mother snapped. "Get out and leave us in peace. You have done enough to hurt us all."

"Come with me, Becky." Victoria stretched out her hand.

Rebecca took a step toward her at the same time that her mother, whether by accident or deliberately, tilted forwards in her chair and pitched out. Rebecca caught her just in time, and her mother clung to her, breathing heavily. Rebecca glanced up at her sister, and Victoria understood she had made her decision. What she didn't realize was that it would be the last time she ever saw her.

CHAPTER 3

Hancock seemed as calm as always, even if that was only ever a surface-deep appearance. Victoria had arrived after a journey that had taken an entire week, thanks to her blue sedan being so temperamental. The car was holding out now, she thought, but she still crossed her fingers superstitiously before opening the window to breathe in the fresh air.

"It seems so peaceful. Too peaceful," she said to herself. Accustomed to the pace of Chicago, she had forgotten how green and tranquil her hometown could be. She drove through the streets, trying to regain her bearings, slowly remembering the landmarks of her childhood. She purposefully avoided her mother's house, and the tightness around her throat relaxed as she bypassed the turnoff and headed instead past Sarah's Hat Boxes. Rebecca had loved wandering through the shop when she was little, admiring the colorful array of recycled hat boxes. She had come home very proudly on her seventh birthday having bought an Alice in Wonderland box, custom-made with a Cheshire cat on the front, Victoria remembered, feeling a tug in her chest.

Unlike Chicago, where all humanity pulsed in time to the same busyness, continually on the go, day and night, here in Hancock, the population had, by this point in the day, settled into a mellow pace. Several residents were ambling out and about with their dogs, reveling in the summer sunshine, while almost as many were relaxing in their gardens, throwing balls to children or grandchildren, or chattering to neighbors. The maples were plumping out their green plumage in the summer wind, bearing no hint of the glorious fall golds and reds to come.

It was incredible that such an apparently tranquil place could have been the scene of her sister's murder. Victoria turned off at Hancock Congregational Church. The church, which also served as Hancock's Meeting House, was a Federal-style building with a lyre-shaped weathervane. It was even harder to believe that her sister's memorial had been held there just two days before, as the apologetic pastor explained when she went inside to find out when it would be.

"My mother hasn't been answering her phone, so I thought I would come directly to the church to find out," a white-lipped Victoria said to the pastor.

"I begged her to postpone till you arrived," the pastor said. "I'm so sorry."

Sorry. Victoria wondered whether she would ever hear that word from her mother. She tried phoning her again when she returned to her car, but Vera's cell phone was off. Again.

"Coward," Victoria shouted at her phone. She flung it down onto the seat next to her. *You could have phoned me. Messaged me. Even asked the pastor to call. Why, Mom? Why?*

She drove the streets, until she had calmed down enough to check in at the Hancock Inn.

"You look exhausted," the girl behind the inn desk exclaimed, as she took Victoria's bags.

Victoria was, but not even the four-poster bed or handmade quilt could entice sleep. Whenever she closed her eyes, her sister's image rose up before her. So instead, she walked across to the Main Street Cheese farm and shop to the left of the inn.

Victoria entered the garden. "Hey! Vicky!" a voice shouted.

"Janet! What are you doing here?" Victoria recognized her old school friend.

"Buying goat's cheese. What else?" Janet replied. Several goats wandered up to them, jostling one another playfully in their attempt to greet the new visitors. In spite of her exhaustion, Victoria felt her spirits lifting, and she put out a hesitant hand to the smallest goat, which butted her excitedly.

Janet Mitchley was as square and solid and blunt as ever, her straight blonde hair still falling into her eyes no matter how often it was pinned or tucked back. "Man, I was devastated to hear about Rebecca." She put her arms around Victoria. "Sorry, I forgot. You're not the hugging type." She stood back and brushed off Victoria's shoulders self-consciously as though trying to undo the embrace.

Victoria couldn't help smiling. "From you, hugs are always okay." She glanced down at Janet's brightly colored skirts, which trailed the ground as she walked. "That's new," she commented, pointing to the tattoo on Janet's ankle that peeped out as she moved.

Janet lifted the hem of her skirt slightly for Victoria to admire the artwork, which consisted of the word "Harvey" in swirling black cursive, followed by a heart. "My son," said Janet proudly. She pointed to the other ankle. "And my daughter, Carrie. I married Blake — you know, his mom used to help out at the library. Do you have a husband and kids?"

Victoria shook her head, sitting down on the grass and kicking off her shoes to avoid discussing the subject further.

"Still time," her friend said, undeterred.

"I hope not," Victoria retorted.

"You don't want to settle down?"

"I have settled down," Victoria replied. "I own an apartment in Chicago. It's not going anywhere. To me, that's far more settled than a man who can up and leave any time he feels like it."

"Cynical. I like it," said Janet. She flopped down next to Victoria. "The cheese can wait. I want to hear how you are doing. I've been thinking of you ever since we heard about Rebecca and wondered if you'd head this way. When you missed the memorial service, I wasn't so sure."

Victoria tried not to cry. "I would have given anything to be here. It took me several days longer than planned to drive up here. Car trouble," she said. "When I arrived, I discovered my mother had already decided to go ahead without me. She didn't even consult me. Just assumed I wasn't going to make it. It felt like she didn't even want me here."

She plucked randomly at a few pieces of grass and watched them scatter in the wind.

"It seems so unreal," she said.

Janet nodded. "To everyone here too." She drew up her legs under her chin so she could rest her head on her knees. "Why would anyone want to kill someone as gentle and beautiful as Rebecca? It just doesn't make sense."

Victoria gazed blankly across the garden, seeing in her mind's eye a younger Rebecca racing across the garden to feed the goats, her auburn hair loose down to her waist, bucket banging against her leg as she ran.

"You don't know — she didn't ever mention anyone who, I don't know, had a grudge against her or didn't get on with her? Maybe a fellow nurse at work or something?" asked Victoria.

"Come on, this is Rebecca we're talking about," protested Janet. "I mean, she even got on with your mother, who is a self-obsessed nutjob. No offense," she added belatedly. Then she stopped. "Although you know," she added slowly, "now you come to mention it, she told me a few weeks back she had had a very difficult time at work. Something to do with an old woman who was ill and her family, I think? Anyway, the old lady died, and the family is trying to sue the hospital for negligence."

Victoria frowned. "That would have stressed her out. Do you know whether Rebecca had a serious boyfriend? She hadn't mentioned anything to me."

Janet thought for a moment.

"She always had someone chasing after her, but you know Rebecca — she never talked much about the men who were interested, mainly because she never gave the attention a thought, especially with your mom being such a pain in the— so demanding."

"Yes, Rebecca could be very forgiving."

"She was *naive*, Vicky. There is a difference. Beautiful, innocent, academic — and naive. I don't think she was aware of the feelings she awoke in just about every guy who met her. Or realized how dangerous those feelings could be."

"What are you talking about?" Victoria was startled.

"Don't you remember how that little creep Joe Evans used to follow her around? He cornered her in the street and said he wouldn't let her go till she had promised to go out with him."

"Oh, yes! I would have murdered him if Steve hadn't done such a good job of half-killing him first," Victoria remembered. "I screamed for him to help me pull Joe away. Steve hit him so hard he ended up in hospital with broken ribs and a fractured nose. He had a real temper!" She shook her head. "I wonder what happened to Steve? He pitched up here out of the blue the year my parents divorced. Everyone thought we were so cool to have a friend who had finished high school. And then my mom got her claws into him. I don't know what she said, but he made some excuse about having to work through some family issues and left Hancock. Even back then she was insanely possessive of us."

Janet stood up and dusted off her skirt. "Steve's back," she said. She glanced at Victoria. "Have you seen him? You guys have a lot in common now."

"What do you mean?"

"You didn't hear he went into law enforcement and he's been made a detective recently?"

Victoria shook her head.

"Not only that," Janet continued, "but he's been assigned to your sister's case. I guess you guys will be seeing a lot more of each other very soon."

CHAPTER 4

"So, how's the rookie feeling?" Officer Karen Timms teased the man opposite her at Hancock Police Department. "Your first homicide."

Detective Steve McCade didn't answer her for a moment.

She came closer to his desk. "Scared?" she asked.

The young man rose from his seat, towering above the petite officer before him. Powerfully built, with blonde hair shaved to a buzz cut and a gun holster on his hip, his face was dominated by a slightly bent nose, the result of his teenage kickboxing career.

"No leads so far," he replied. "It could have been anyone who killed Rebecca Wharton. Classic cold-case material."

Karen frowned.

"I hope, for Vera's sake, you are wrong. My daughter Claire used to play with her twins, Rebecca and—"

"Victoria," Steve interrupted, giving the skew smile that Karen was sure was the reason for her grown-up daughter's sudden interest in her mother's work. "Claire was a few years behind the twins at school, right?"

Karen nodded. "Victoria was quite an intense girl, I recall. She was forever in the library as a child. I can just picture that mop of dark curly hair half-hidden behind a big book. According to my son, at least, she still had that gorgeous hair after she'd grown up, and nice legs to boot. I guess it will feel strange working together with her on the case," she continued, preparing to head out. She was stopped by a powerful hand on her shoulder.

"What do you mean?" Steve demanded, blocking her way.

"Victoria phoned a couple of days ago, when you were on leave, and the chief of police has said you two will be collaborating on the case. Didn't you get his message? It seems Victoria is highly thought of as a detective in Chicago. She's staying at the Hancock Inn. Here's her number. You need to get in contact with her."

Steve bit his lip thoughtfully, his eyes never leaving Karen's. "She's a detective then?" he said, his expression hard to read. "And she's been given permission by the Chief to investigate her own sister's murder? How did she wangle that?"

"Yes, it's a conflict of interest, but wouldn't you demand to be seconded to the investigation if it were your sister? Plus, she's one of the best. It's said she never gives up."

Steve entered the number Karen had given him into his phone. "Never gives up? Doesn't she have family waiting for her in Chicago?"

Before Karen could answer, they were interrupted by a knock on the door.

"I'm single, if that answers your question," replied Victoria, entering the room.

She thought a smile flitted across Steve's mouth, but it was gone so quickly she couldn't be sure. The fuller face she remembered had slimmed down, leaving a hardened jawline and lean cheeks. The casualness of his oversized sweaters was gone, discarded for the formality of a buttoned work shirt, which, though fitting well around his waist, was too narrow for the breadth of his shoulders.

"Good to see you again, Steve, Karen. I just wanted to check in and let you know I'm here." She looked at Steve.

"I've been driving most of the day, so I thought we could meet tomorrow morning to discuss my sister's case?"

"Sure," Steve replied. "Whenever suits you. I can come by the inn."

"You have our full support, Victoria," Karen said. "If anyone can discover who did this to your sister, it is you. Your boss sent on this to us." She held out several stapled pages to Vicky, who took them, maintaining the slight distance that she always kept between herself and her colleagues.

"What's this?"

"Your transfer reference. You're a heroine for the work you did with gangs in the 11th District while you were a cop."

"The heart of Chi-raq," murmured Steve.

"Don't call Chicago that," Victoria snapped, defending the city she had come to call home.

"It wasn't me. You know why rappers named it that?"

"Of course. It was in *Time* magazine — in the year the article was written, the overall homicide rates of Chicago and Iraq were seventeen and twenty per one hundred thousand respectively." She reeled off the figures effortlessly. "In the 11th District, the homicide rate was higher than in Iraq." Her eyes looked beyond him briefly as she recalled the faces, so many of them, of the families she had worked with.

"You're too young to be married to your work, Detective," Steve said, smiling ironically.

"It's always been faithful to me," Victoria sighed, tossing down the papers in her hand. "Until now, that is."

CHAPTER 5

Victoria groaned as the alarm on her phone beeped. She put out a hand to switch it off and sat up groggily, wishing the night had brought the rest she needed. A dull ache sat behind her eyes, and she fumbled in her drawer for the headache tablets she always kept with her. She glanced out of the window. It was light already, the sky an early-morning grayish blue.

"Fresh air," she said firmly, pulling her hair into a ponytail. She had more than enough time to go out before her meeting with Steve, she told herself, glancing at her phone. After quickly downing her tablet, she pulled on a T-shirt and some sweatpants and stuck her sunglasses on her forehead before shoving her phone in her pocket and heading outdoors.

Once outside, she took a deep breath, her brain clearing in the morning air. She walked past the red-bricked Main Street Cheese she had visited the day before, its white-painted windows all still closed. The sidewalk was almost clear of the leafy layer that covered the path in the fall, and the streets were quiet.

Automatically, born of long practice, she started heading in the direction of her family home. It was only when her head started aching that she realized she was clenching her jaw.

She felt in her pocket for her phone, and her index and middle fingers tapped out a nervous drumbeat on the screen.

"Just try calling her again," she chided herself. "The worst she can do is answer."

Victoria took out her phone and pulled up her mother's number. The phone rang several times before cutting off abruptly. Victoria felt as though she had been slapped. Her shoulders slumped, though whether from disappointment or relief she wasn't sure. Maybe it was both. She shrugged to herself and headed back toward the inn.

"Coffee!" she muttered as she pushed through the door. "Strong coffee." A few minutes later, she was sinking into a chair in the living room of the Hancock Inn, her hands cupped around her mug to warm them. She stared ahead of her, bleary-eyed, her hair — whipped wild by the wind — falling in her face.

"Not a morning person, I take it?" Glancing up, she found Steve McCade right in front of her, looking indecently awake and alert for so early in the day. Victoria hastily tried to straighten her hair into some sort of order. Amused, he sat beside her and leaned across to brush a strand from her eyes.

She drew back at the unexpected gesture. "Steve, hi," she replied lightly, hoping her cheeks were not as red as they felt. "I wasn't expecting you so early. Excuse the bed hair! A combination of a bad sleep and a walk in the Hancock wind. I've just got back." She swallowed. "My sister and I used to come to the inn when we were younger. I didn't quite believe she was dead until I arrived yesterday and she didn't come rushing through the red door."

"You're staying here for the duration of the case, then? Not with your mom?"

Victoria got the feeling he was watching her closely. She laughed humorlessly. "You think my mother would have welcomed me with open arms? She didn't even wait for me to arrive before she held the memorial. Doesn't answer my calls." She shook her head, then put down her coffee and got up. "I'd better go and get some breakfast. Then I thought

I'd head along to the library. One of the volunteers who is assisting with the family story time they have on Thursdays is apparently the jogger who found my sister's body?"

Steve nodded. "Paula Gardner, a retired English teacher. You don't need to see her — I've spoken to her already. The interview is in your sister's file. But like I said, she really had nothing to add. You'll also see that we went through your sister's apartment and got a forensic report both from there and from the crime scene, but there wasn't really anything of significance in either report. Although one thing that may be valuable is that a few fingerprints found on your sister's body match those on a beer bottle from the murder scene."

"When can I see the file?" Victoria demanded.

He shrugged. "Any time, but looking at it is not even worth your time, believe me. There are really no leads at present."

"I've got to try," she replied. "I loved my sister."

"I cared about Becky too," he said.

She stared at him blankly. Her sister never allowed anyone but those closest to her to call her that. She took a step closer, trying to read his thoughts. Exactly how close had he been to her sister?

CHAPTER 6

Paula Gardner had been buttonholed at the library by one of the mothers, who was keen to gossip.

"Everyone knew who Rebecca *was*, of course, but none of us really *knew* her," the sharp-faced mom of two screaming toddlers was saying, oblivious to the glares of those trying to read.

"She kept very much to herself." Paula, a round, contented woman with neatly cropped gray-blonde hair, picked up the Gruffalo book she had selected in the hopes her companion would stop talking. No such luck.

"I bet there was a boyfriend involved. I've heard the rumors."

Victoria slipped in behind a group of moms in time to overhear the words.

"*Apparently*," said the sharp-faced mother, "there was not just one guy after her but two. Who knows, probably more."

Paula Gardner did not like gossiping, but she was intrigued. She opened her mouth to ask whose name Rebecca's had been linked to, then her better judgment prevailed and she closed her mouth again.

Victoria took cautious a step forward. Neither woman even noticed her presence.

"I saw her with someone else recently. Right across the road from here."

"It could have been anyone."

"He was carrying her shopping bags for her, a broad-shouldered man in his twenties, with a small scar on his face. Curly coppery hair."

Paula stared at the woman uneasily, giving her full attention for the first time.

"What sort of a — where was the scar?" she asked, trying to sound casual.

"It curved over his jaw."

Paula slammed the book shut.

"Nonsense. You couldn't possibly have seen that detail from across the street," Paula snapped, losing her composure. "I'm sorry. I think I'm going to start reading my book now."

"Just a moment. Mrs Gardner?" Victoria stepped forward. Paula started at the sound of her voice.

"I'm Detective Victoria Wharton, sister to Rebecca."

The sharp-faced woman beat a hasty retreat, and Paula stretched out her hand to Victoria in greeting. "I suppose you overheard all that," she said in embarrassment.

Victoria nodded. "I hear you discovered my sister's body. Do you have a moment before story time begins?"

Paula nodded and gestured to Victoria to go outside with her where they could speak in private. They stood at the top of the steps leading up to the entrance. Victoria shifted away from the large red-, white- and-blue flag on the door and looked at the woman beside her. "Could you tell me what happened, Mrs Gardner?"

"I was taking the dogs for a walk early on Friday morning. I set off from the Harris Center and did one of the East Side trails. It's good exercise through hardwood forest but not too strenuous. I was expecting it to be busy, but I guess after the rains the night before, people thought it might be too wet. The dogs started barking at something off the trail, not far from the Harris Center."

Paula sighed and took off her glasses to wipe her eyes. "It was then I discovered your sister's body, behind some rocks. I had left my phone in the car, and I hurried back to call the police. Detective McCade responded with another officer — I didn't catch his name — and met me at my car. The officer escorted me home."

"Was there any chance she might have fallen? I mean, are you sure she was murdered?"

Paula shook her head. "Her head was injured," she said with difficulty, "as if she had been hit with something heavy. It didn't look like an accident."

"And no evidence of—" Victoria hesitated — "any other motive?"

"I don't know. Her cell phone was with her, so it didn't look like it had been a mugging or something."

Victoria looked at her squarely. "Did you know her at all?"

"Slightly, yes, I— by sight, I did. My family moved here recently, a few years after my retirement, so I didn't know her well, but we would smile and greet each other if we passed. She was always warm and friendly. There was an innocence about her."

"Yes," replied Victoria slowly, staring at her hands. *Innocent.* What had Janet called her? *Naive.*

"The woman you were talking to when I arrived mentioned a young man? With a scar, she said?"

Paula looked flustered. "She must be mistaken," she said. "She's just a troublemaker."

"Why do you say that?" Victoria asked.

"Because that description only fits one person in this town," replied Paula. "And that's John."

"John?"

"John Gardner," Paula replied. "We moved here to be closer to him. He's my son."

CHAPTER 7

"Steve, Victoria, look at this," Officer Karen Timms called.

Steve strode across the room and leaned over Karen, peering at her screen, his broad back blocking the sunlight.

"Look at this Facebook profile."

"Rebecca Wharton? I've checked it already. Why would you do that?"

Victoria came through at this, and Steve glanced up at her, smiling slightly and holding her gaze for a moment. A faint smile line curved invitingly around the corner of his mouth, she noticed, and she suppressed an unbidden desire to touch his face. *Becky. He had called her sister Becky.* The thought kept churning through her mind, reminding her, as though she needed reminding, never to trust anyone. Don't let anyone close. But even as she thought it, she realized with annoyance she was smiling back.

"Curiosity," said Karen. "Look at all these posts on her wall from Megan Jenkins."

She pointed to one as she read. "*Hey Rebecca. Thought you would identify with this.*"

"It's just a cartoon about a nurse accidentally swapping patient charts," Victoria shrugged. "And there's another one about a nurse who messed up medication for a patient. Quite funny actually."

"Not if Megan Jenkins is the daughter of Winifred Hulbert," said Karen. She pointed to a link to an obituary. It had been shared by Megan — again on Rebecca's wall.

"Click on the link to the full obituary," snapped Victoria. She leaned forward as the article popped up. They read in silence, then stared at each other.

Victoria shook her head. "Janet, my friend, mentioned the other day that my sister had had a patient who died and whose family were causing legal trouble," she said. "Sounds like it wasn't just the hospital they were after. Look at all these cartoons."

"Why would your sister be friends with someone like that?" asked Karen.

Victoria shrugged. "She was very gentle. Patients and their families often looked her up on social media, and she was too kind-hearted not to accept their friend requests." She sighed. "But these cartoons amount to threats. I didn't see anything about Megan Jenkins in Rebecca's file. It's definitely an angle to be added."

Steve McCade placed a hand on her shoulder. Her usual instinct was to draw back, but another part of her rebelled, and she felt a brief longing to lose herself in his arms.

He smiled. "Are you finished with your sister's file?"

His proximity was distracting. She couldn't think.

"Yeah, I guess so. It says in the file that according to my mother, a scarf was missing from her apartment that wasn't found with her body?"

"Maybe she had lost it?"

Victoria stepped back, trying to remember what else it was that had bothered her. Steve's smile faded as she paused.

"I wanted to ask you — why was robbery mentioned as a possible motive?"

"Simple. Because her phone was taken. We searched her home, and it wasn't there, and when we dialed the number your mom gave us, it went straight to voicemail."

"But that's crazy," Victoria exploded, exhaustion making her speak more harshly than she intended. "I spoke to Paula Gardner, and she said Rebecca had her cell phone with her."

"Why did you speak to Paula when I'd already done so?" demanded Steve. She sensed that he was struggling not to lose his temper and felt an involuntary shiver of something — was it fear? She shook it off.

"Are you checking to see if I slipped up? Have another look at your sister's file. Paula Gardner left the body and returned to her car to call us. By the time I got there, the phone was gone."

Victoria stared at him.

"You mean the murderer was interrupted by Paula Gardner before he could steal the phone, and hid until she left?"

"Yeah, looks like it. Her empty wallet was found a short distance away from the body, and Paula didn't recall seeing that when she found the body either. There's been a dodgy character hanging around Hancock the past month or two, apparently a homeless war veteran with a drinking problem. A few of the people we spoke to claimed they saw a beggar near the Harris Center on the day your sister's body was found."

Victoria shook her head. "It just doesn't make sense. The preliminary autopsy results say my sister was attacked late on Thursday evening or very early Friday and died shortly afterwards. By the time her body was found, the murderer would have been long gone."

"Or the murderer was disturbed by someone and so came back later to accomplish his aim of stealing from her," Karen said.

"I need her phone records," said Victoria, walking back and forth by the window. "And I have to speak to Megan to find out more about the court case. I don't believe the motive behind my sister's death was robbery. Beggar or not. Not here in Hancock. Maybe someone who had nothing to do with the crime found the phone and took it."

"I'll get the phone records," said Steve. "You speak to Megan."

He reached out a hand to stop Victoria pacing, and she turned to see him smiling disquietingly at her, the anger in his eyes replaced by an emotion she couldn't quite place.

"Shall we call it a truce, Detective Wharton?" he said.

She withdrew but couldn't resist the smile. She had just been alone for too long, she told herself, aware for the first time in ages that it was loneliness she had felt, even in Chicago, when she had thought she was doing so well. She was aware of a latent excitement, and her heart raced with anxiety.

"Fine," she said coolly, hoping neither Steve nor Karen could see through her veneer of bravado. "Let's call it a truce."

CHAPTER 8

Victoria stepped out of her car, gazing up in awe at the size of the country residence before her and the wealth that had clearly been lavished on its upkeep. Situated on the outskirts of Hancock, it was a triple-storied mansion in the nineteenth-century Italianate style, with broad green eaves providing a contrast to the white-painted clapboard walls. It boasted a front gable and a series of arched windows, the panes gleaming as if they had just been polished.

Victoria was greeted at the door by a surly-faced teenager, who reluctantly admitted he was Gavin Jenkins and even more reluctantly agreed to fetch his mother. He left Victoria waiting in the hallway. She was contemplating the impressive staircase, one hand on the banister when a small, wiry woman burst in, clearly overwrought.

"I'm Vict—" Victoria started.

"What do you want?" the woman interrupted. "More photographs, I suppose? I've said everything I wanted to say." She looked over at her son, still hanging around. "You needn't wait, Gavin," she said coldly. "I'm sure you have homework to do."

He stared at her resentfully before slouching off.

"What newspaper are you from?" the woman asked Victoria.

"I'm a detective. Investigating the murder of Rebecca Wharton. Are you Mrs Megan Jenkins?"

It was the woman's turn to stare at her, and her face whitened. "Won't you come through and sit down?" she said, more courteously. "Yes, yes, I'm — we heard, of course. It was murder?"

Victoria nodded, following her into a wood-lined living room that was larger than Victoria's entire apartment. A fireplace was built into the wall, and large French windows looked out onto a lawn of grass that had been manicured into submission by some agricultural artist.

"I noticed your Facebook posts to Rebecca," Victoria said.

Before she could continue, a dark-haired, heavy-set man entered the room, a riding whip in his hand. He was middle-aged but attractive in a rather overbearing way. Probably used to using his looks to get his way, Victoria thought cynically.

"Are you bothering my wife?" he growled through a thick moustache. He stalked over to her. "We've had journalists annoying us all week trying to find out about our lawsuit. Don't you think it's time you focused on another story?"

"Like the murder of Rebecca Wharton?" suggested Victoria. She smiled tightly. "I'm Detective Victoria Wharton."

"Wharton," repeated Megan. "Are you related to Rebecca then?"

"Her sister," Victoria replied tersely, turning to Megan's husband. "And you must be Maurice Jenkins?"

"That's right." Megan took her husband's arm and drew him to a plush armchair.

"Detective?" The man glared at her. "That's what we need to uncover the truth about my mother-in-law's death."

Victoria was grateful to see him drop the riding whip on the carpet.

"My mother went into hospital with a leg infection and ended up dead," said Megan.

Victoria nodded. She had gone to the hospital first, and the doctor had spoken at length about the pending lawsuit.

"I understand she had decided against the operation the hospital staff wanted to do," said Victoria. "And as a result, she developed gangrene."

"It was horrible!" exclaimed Megan, her temporary calmness giving way to agitation. "We begged the hospital time and again to let her take the medication she had always taken for infections of that kind."

"From what I was told, though, her circulation had deteriorated, so the medication was no longer effective, even though they apparently tried it?"

"Total garbage," said Megan, her voice rising shrilly. "The nurses kept trying to give her other concoctions and to force her to agree to being opened up and having stents put in."

Victoria lifted her eyebrows. "To allow the circulation to reach the infection, so that the medication would be effective?"

"Completely unnecessary," said Megan. "If they had just allowed her more time on her medication she would be here today."

"The case notes indicate that once the infection set in, the hospital had to operate to amputate the gangrenous part of the leg."

"And my mother-in-law died from the shock of the amputation," Maurice Jenkins said. Though he was attempting to inject anger into his voice, Victoria was aware of a strange undercurrent in his tone. But why? She frowned. *What are you hiding, Maurice?*

"What did this have to do with Rebecca, my sister?" asked Victoria. "The administrators say she was often the nurse on duty while your mom was in hospital?"

Megan nodded, her head bobbing as her emotions got ahead of her words. "We thought at first she was different from the others," she said. "She seemed so kind and gentle. But in the end," she added, her teeth gritted, "she was just the same as the others. Insisting that my mother subject her body to dangerous operations instead of just treating her with the medicine we knew would work."

"That's right," Maurice said. "It was completely irresponsible of her."

"And so you blamed her when your mother-in-law died, Mr. Jenkins?"

Maurice glanced uneasily at his wife. "The word 'blame' is a strong one," he said awkwardly, "but there is no doubt there was negligence involved."

"And so you sent threatening images to her Facebook page?" Victoria said quietly to Megan, who shifted in her seat and fidgeted with her hands before answering.

"I would hardly call cartoons threatening," she said evasively.

"But the message was clear. You intended to let my sister know you blamed her."

"Well, if the glove fits . . ." Megan shrugged. "If her actions were above board, she had no need to feel guilty or to let the cartoons bother her."

"And where were you last Thursday evening and Friday morning, which we've established was the time of Rebecca's death?" asked Victoria, leaning forward. "You didn't decide to do one of the walks from the Harris Center?"

"We do sometimes, but I don't believe we did then . . ." Megan trailed off.

"Actually, I think we might have on Friday," said Maurice, "but later in the day. Much later. We had an appointment with our lawyer about the hospital case." He leaned a little closer toward Victoria. "What happened to your sister?" he asked.

"She sustained head injuries," Victoria replied. "Her body was found along one of the hiking trails."

She stood up.

"That's all, thanks," she said. "If you think of anything that might be relevant, I'm staying at the Hancock Inn."

Megan rose too and came across to her, clutching her elbow as they left the room ahead of Maurice. Victoria stepped back instinctively, removing her arm, only to have Megan clutch her again. Out of the corner of her eyes, Victoria caught sight of Gavin in the distance, a sardonic sneer on his face, and wondered whether he had overheard the conversation. Her attention returned to Megan.

"We had nothing to do with her murder," she said, lifting lined eyes to Victoria's then turning to her husband for affirmation. "We never even saw her after my mother's death — did we, Maurice?"

CHAPTER 9

Early on Saturday, Janet walked through the entrance of the Hancock Inn, hoping to find Victoria. There was no sign of her in the dining room. She dodged around a cluster of early risers about to leave the breakfast table, and flagged down one of the servers.

"I haven't seen her yet. Check her room. You know the way? Straight down the passage, the room at the very end."

Janet knocked loudly on Victoria's door, and on hearing a stifled gasp, walked in on Victoria, sitting straight up in her four-poster bed, her hand to her chest and her face white.

"Vicky!" Janet hurried forward and dropped down onto the bed. "You look like you've seen a ghost."

Victoria managed a laugh and fumbled for her water on the bedside table.

"Several," she muttered, taking a sip of water. "I thought the nightmares were in the past." Her hand fluttered to her chest again as she inhaled deeply to regulate her breathing.

"Your father?" Janet asked, gently taking the glass of water from her friend's shaking hand.

Victoria nodded.

"And then when I heard you knocking and you walked in, I thought for a moment—" She managed a smile. "And my mother still blames me. Says that I destroyed her marriage. Even though it was long dead. I can never remember a time when they seemed happy together. I don't know what happened. I've often wondered."

Janet patted Victoria's hand, careful not to infringe too much on her space. "You know damn well if he'd stayed, he would have been found guilty and imprisoned, and her marriage would have been over anyway. What he did was unforgivable."

"Yes. You know, if I hadn't reported him, he would have done the same thing to Rebecca." She sank her head onto her drawn-up knees. "I was trying to protect her."

"You did protect her," Janet said gently. "And yourself." She smiled at her friend, then stood up, flinging open the curtains. "You're coming with me," she said. "Get dressed. You have five minutes."

"Where are we going?" Victoria protested.

"You remember the Historical Society, don't you? It's their annual plant sale."

Victoria groaned as she plodded to the bathroom, but Janet wasn't taking no for an answer.

"And don't tell me you have to work," she shouted through the closed door, "because it is the weekend, and you need to rest."

Twenty minutes later, Janet was dragging her reluctant friend around the plant sale.

"At least they sell food too," Victoria mumbled through a mouthful of Karen Timms's cheesecake.

"Stop whining," ordered Janet. "No one can enjoy cake as much as you've been enjoying that and still complain. Just look at the plants around you, breathe in all the oxygen they're releasing."

"Who's whining?" Victoria heard a voice behind her ask, and an oddly familiar face grinned at her.

"This one," Janet said to the man who had spoken, poking Victoria with her finger. He was standing behind a table brimming with chocolate cakes, the icing cascading temptingly down the sides. "How are you, John?"

Of course. John Gardner, son of Paula. No wonder she thought she had seen his face before. There was the healing scar curving over his jaw, and his head was topped by short copper curls. Powerful shoulders. Friendly smile yet sad eyes, she noted, wondering fleetingly what made them so wistful.

"Did you make these?" Victoria asked, hoping to engage him in conversation. It wasn't difficult. He was clearly bored.

"I wish. I've been too busy down at the surgery, but my mom made them, and I offered to help her out for a few minutes while she was busy."

"Surgery? Are you a doctor?" Victoria asked in surprise.

"Veterinarian. I've started a practice here recently," he said. "Are you new here?"

Victoria hesitated for a moment then put out her hand and said, "Detective Victoria Wharton. I'm with the Chicago police but staying at the Hancock Inn while I investigate the murder of my sister, Rebecca. I understand you were friends?"

Did she notice a wariness creep into his eyes? She couldn't be sure.

"Right. I'm so sorry about your loss."

"Perhaps we could chat later?"

"We can chat now," he said, coming around the table. His mother had returned. He took Victoria by the elbow and steered her through the crowds.

Janet waved at her. "Catch up later," she mouthed.

Victoria shook off his hand. "Please don't touch me," she said, annoyed at, rather than threatened by, his proximity.

He dropped his hand and looked thoughtfully at her. "This place is crawling with people. Shall we speak at my surgery?"

* * *

"I'm not sure it's much quieter after all," he said with a grin a few minutes later. An overgrown St. Bernard leaped up at them enthusiastically at the door. "This is St. Patrick. Not a patient, just a nuisance who invited himself to stay and hasn't left."

John led her through to his rooms, closely followed by St. Patrick.

"No, don't shut him out," Victoria said nervously as John tried to close the door. The room was neat and sterile with several qualification certificates on the wall and one other framed page that appeared to be a poem.

"Sure."

John left the door open so that the big dog could wander in and out. He indicated the seat closest to the exit. She took it with relief, and he smiled at her. He had a small dimple in his cheek, just above the scar.

"You're much closer to the door than I am," he reassured her. "You can always make a bolt for it if you think I'm dangerous."

"I didn't—"

"Yeah, you did. You checked all possible exits. It's not a problem."

She stared at her hands, thrown off track. This wasn't how she'd expected the interview to go. "Are you always this frank?" she asked, trying to hide her embarrassment.

"Often," he said. "Not always. I mean, I didn't tell anyone your sister and I were friends."

"Just friends?"

He reached for a packet of dog biscuits and tossed one to St. Patrick.

"Yes, not my choice." He shrugged. "I was really keen on her. She was beautiful and had an unworldly quality about her, I guess."

"An innocence," nodded Victoria. "Everyone says so. Also that she was naive."

"Is that so wrong? I mean, it's pretty unusual to have that sort of outlook on the world, especially these days."

"It can be dangerous."

He stared at her. "What do you mean?"

Victoria tried to articulate the picture she was starting to build up. "I mean that she didn't always understand people's true motives. She was intelligent, but she was so genuine herself that it could blind her to less honorable motives in others. She accepted a friend request from a patient's daughter on Facebook and ended up being on the receiving end of online threats. It could also make her vulnerable in her relationships with men."

"Such as myself?" John asked.

"Possibly, yes." If he was going to be frank, why shouldn't she? "She hardly even seemed to notice how attracted to her men were. Treated everyone with the same kindness and friendliness but—"

John laughed ruefully. "That's true. I never felt like I made any headway in our relationship. I took her flowers, lent her books I had bought because I thought she'd enjoy them, invited her on walks, but in the end, I just realized we were going to be friends and nothing more. Her whole focus was elsewhere."

"My mother?" asked Victoria.

"Yeah," he nodded. "She wouldn't even let me meet her. Apparently she is really sickly."

"And controlling." Victoria hadn't meant to say it, but it slipped out. "Rebecca was all she had once I left, and she was grimly determined not to let her out of her grasp. Rebecca messaged me often, although we hadn't seen each other for ages. My mother used to fly into . . . abusive rages, if she suspected anyone was overly friendly with Becky. She once even smashed a plate on the floor. My sister learned the hard way to keep quiet about her relationships, however innocent they were." Victoria bit her lip. "And now she's gone."

He hesitated, looking for a moment far more like a vulnerable little boy than the confident young vet before her. "There is a hike this Saturday that I'm doing."

"Right," she said.

He caught her eye for a moment, and the dimple showed itself. "Do you enjoy hiking?"

She smiled briefly, unable to resist the sudden shyness in his question. "I used to," she said, thinking of how her sister had been found off the trail of one of the East Side walks.

"Yeah," he rushed on. "I go out with this group. I help out Sandy, the facilitator, as a volunteer. It's a support group called 'Hiking through Grief'."

She stared at him for a moment, humiliated to have thought that he wanted to spend time with her and angry with herself for letting down her guard or even contemplating going with him. What was her problem?

"Right," she said. "Well, I tell you what, Dr Gardner, when I need your hiking therapy, I will let you know. Until then, why don't you stick to your job rather than playing psychologist?"

"I didn't mean—"

He walked to the window and stared out in silence, then glanced at the framed page on the wall beside him.

Victoria rose.

"You may be right," he said suddenly, turning around, "about your sister's innocence being dangerous."

He tapped the framed page on the wall. "This is one of my mom's favorite poems, which is why it is hanging on the wall here. She was an English teacher. 'My Last Duchess' by Browning. Do you know it?"

Victoria shook her head.

"Read it some time," he advised. "The narrator is a man writing about his wife, whom he has had assassinated out of jealousy, simply because she didn't favor him above the others she showed kindness to. She reminds me of your sister."

Victoria nodded. "You think the motive could have been jealousy?"

"Perhaps."

She looked thoughtfully at the scar on his jaw, wondering whether he was someone who could be roused to great anger and jealousy. Certainly he would have had the physique to overpower her sister.

"And who would represent the narrator?" she asked pointedly.

She thought she could see amusement in his eyes, though whether it was mocking or not she couldn't be sure.

"If we knew that, we would know who murdered your sister," he replied, showing her out.

CHAPTER 10

Steve was sitting in Fiddleheads Cafe — named after a fern's furled fronds, which resemble the scroll on the neck of a fiddle. He had just picked up his coffee mug, when Karen Timms knocked on the window next to his table. He gave her the lopsided smile that left her daughter tongue-tied and gestured to her to come in.

"Coincidence finding you here," she exclaimed. "I was just wondering whether I should call you. I was down at the station when Rebecca Wharton's cell-phone company phoned your line to say that they had sent through the phone records you asked for."

Steve suddenly stopped smiling and leaned forward, his muscles taut. "And?"

Karen shrugged. "And nothing."

"You didn't see the records?"

"No, of course not. The stuff was emailed directly to you, they said."

"Thanks." Steve threw a few bank notes onto the table and grabbed the jacket he had slung over his chair.

"You're leaving?"

"See you Monday!" he shouted over his shoulder as he ran.

* * *

Victoria sat outside her mother's house in her car, reading 'My Last Duchess' on her phone, mostly to delay going in.

That's my last Duchess painted on the wall . . .

. . . she smiled, no doubt,
Whene'er I passed her; but who passed without
Much the same smile?

Victoria read on, shivering at the chilling lines that describe the murder of the duchess.

I gave commands;
Then all smiles stopped together.

Enough. She looked up at her mother's house. She remembered it as run-down, but she was not prepared for how dilapidated the property had become. The hedge around the garden stood almost six feet high in places, and in others it was browned and withered, the ground littered with dead branches and leaves.

Swallowing down the nausea that arose when she thought of going inside, she forced herself to open the car door and get out. She walked slowly up the garden path and rang the doorbell. No answer, but she noticed the bedroom curtain falling back as though someone behind it had lifted it a fraction. Determined, now that she was actually there, to get the visit over and done with, Victoria knocked loudly on the bedroom window until a reluctant hand drew the curtain back again. Her mother lifted her other hand in greeting, barely making eye contact with her daughter, and the curtain fell. Victoria could hear the sound of her mother's wheelchair moving across the wooden flooring as she made her way to the front door.

"So you finally decided to pay your mother a call." Vera's voice was flat and dull as she unlatched the door. "I was wondering whether you were going to make the effort."

On the attack already. You don't even wait for me to set foot inside, do you? Victoria glanced at the time on her phone. Thank goodness she'd agreed to meet Janet later. It would give her an excuse to get away.

"Whenever I have called there has been no answer," Victoria said.

Vera wheeled herself through to the living room, which was shrouded in darkness. Victoria opened the curtains, letting the sunlight fall on the fading furniture and the unwashed breakfast tray still sitting on a coffee table. The room was scattered with magazines and clutter, and nightmarish memories lurked in every corner.

"When I got here, I learned from the pastor the memorial had already been held," said Victoria. She bit her lip. "Why would you do that? And why haven't you been answering my calls?"

"Everything is always about you, isn't it? Always has been." Her mother laughed drily. "I had to do everything myself when Becky died because you weren't here. As per usual. Select hymns, drive myself to the pastor, talk to the police. I just wanted it all to be over as soon as possible. I even had to view—" She placed her sleeve over her mouth for a moment to stop herself from losing control — "your sister's corpse."

Victoria sank onto the ripped couch, feeling sick. "I'm sorry. I was on my way. My car kept giving trouble, and I tried to call and tell you, repeatedly. I came as fast as I could."

"Not fast enough. All your calls came too late. If you'd been here in the first place, with your family, you wouldn't have had to drive out. You would have been here. Maybe your sister wouldn't have been out alone."

"She wasn't out alone," Victoria replied. "That was the problem."

"Of course she was. She was robbed and left to die."

"Is that what the police told you?" demanded Victoria, feeling her temper rising. She was going to confront Steve about it at the first opportunity. Why did he keep harping on about the idea of a robbery? "It is also possible she was killed by someone she knew. I thought you might have some idea who she had been seeing."

"*Becky* had no secrets from me," her mother said, emphasizing her daughter's name as if to compare her openness with Victoria's absence and silence.

"Did she have any close friends?"

Her mother shrugged. "We were the closest to each other. Becky didn't have much time or desire to socialize. Though she did have a couple of friends that she went out with now and then."

"She didn't still live here, though, did she? She told me she had a place of her own."

"Yes, I don't know why," her mother replied plaintively. "Her room was here. She shouldn't have left. It wasn't necessary, especially seeing she was single. I suggested she move back home."

"I'm sure you did," Victoria said under her breath. "She didn't talk about anyone special, did she?"

"Don't be ridiculous," her mother sneered. "If there had been someone in her life, I would have been the first person she would have told. But men were never her priority, were they?"

"How could they be?" Victoria replied.

Her mother looked at her sharply. "Becky always had her priorities right," she said. "I don't know what I would have done without her. When you drove your father away and took to roaming Hancock in your teens with that young kickboxing hellhound who showed up out of nowhere, she was the only one I could rely on when I needed help."

Victoria tried to shut out the last images she had of her father, but the sickening creak of her bedroom door as he slipped in at night kept echoing through her brain. Only Becky had believed her and given her the strength to go to the police.

"Becky was the only one I could rely on too," she said, half to herself.

"If you knew the pain you have put me through . . ." Vera repeated a well-worn mantra.

"You were never happy even before the divorce," said Victoria. She paused and bit her lip. "Why? What happened?"

Vera swallowed and half opened her mouth as though tempted to speak, but they were interrupted by the ringtone of Victoria's cell phone. She didn't hesitate to answer it.

"Hello? What? So soon? I'm meeting Janet later today, but I can come past your place first. I'll let her know. Where are you living? Right. It's so close by, I'll just walk to you."

"Who was that?" asked her mother, her ears pricking up at the sound of the male voice.

Victoria smiled wryly. "The kickboxing hellhound," she replied as she put her phone away. "Detective Steve McCade. He's got Rebecca's cell-phone records." She felt a small stab of satisfaction as she saw her mother start and added casually, "He wants to meet up with me to discuss them."

"I never liked that boy." Vera's expressionless tone hid, Victoria knew, a seething jumble of jealousy. "I didn't like him at all."

"No, you didn't," said Victoria, her voice equally expressionless.

"He's not good for you," her mother continued, watching each barb sink in. "Keep well away from him. I'm only thinking of your happiness, Victoria."

"I'm sure you are," Victoria replied. "But I happen to be working on the case with him. We are both detectives, Mother. It's purely professional."

"Is it?" Her mother's voice rang in Victoria's ears as she left the house. *Is your relationship with Steve strictly professional?*

CHAPTER 11

Victoria pushed Steve's doorbell then wiped her hand, slightly sticky, on her jeans. The sound of running water came from deep inside the house, then the thudding of bare feet on tiles.

He put his head around the front door, his hair damp and smelling faintly of shampoo.

"That was quick," he said, standing back to let her in. She blushed as she saw he was still in a towel. "I wasn't expecting you yet."

"I'll wait outside." She pulled back, embarrassed, but he took her arm, drawing her a little closer as he closed the door. She felt breathless and slightly giddy. She slipped under his arm and stood back, clutching her handbag. "I was at my mother's house," she said, scarcely aware of what she was saying. "We were just talking about you."

"Right," he said, his light-heartedness dissipating and eyes watchful. "Your mother loves me almost as much as I do her."

"Almost." She smiled, watching a drop of water weave its way down his cheek and slide down his neck. She sighed. "She and I have never got on either."

Steve grimaced. "Like my mom and me," he replied. "Single mom. Always too busy for me. Never too busy to drink though."

"What about your dad?" Victoria asked. "You've never mentioned him."

Steve's smile was grim, his expression unfathomable. "What was there to tell?" he said. "I never knew him. Maybe if he had been around, things would have been different." He frowned as though he were annoyed with himself for revealing so much. "That's life, I guess. Want anything to drink?"

Victoria shook her head. "You said you've got the phone records?"

He nodded and gestured to her to sit, removing the gun holster he always wore at work from the couch.

"Give me a second to change. Make yourself at home."

He disappeared into his bedroom. Victoria quickly messaged Janet to let her know where she was in case the visit took longer than expected. She put her phone away and looked around. Steve's living room was everything her mother's wasn't: clean, neat, everything in its place. It was clearly the room of a man who knew what he wanted and where he wanted it. A large frame holding several photos stood on one wall. She rose and gazed at the pictures. In one fading photo in the corner of the frame, there was a group of laughing youngsters. In the middle of the group stood Steve, one arm around her and the other around Becky, who smiled out of the photo, her face so young and eager that it broke Victoria's heart.

She sat on the black leather couch, lost in the past, until Steve emerged a few minutes later, pulling on his shirt. She looked away quickly, noting the slight smile as he saw her embarrassment.

"So, business," she said formally. "Tell me about the records."

He nodded, tossing his wet towel over the back of the couch.

"Your sister made and received a few calls here and there but not many. The library. The hospital. Until three weeks ago." He passed her a piece of paper on which he had jotted down a number.

"Does this look familiar at all?"

"No, should it?"

He grimaced. "I rang it just now. John Gardner. The vet. Turns out he phoned your sister every day for the twenty-one days leading up to her death."

John. Victoria glanced at him, startled.

"I spoke to John today," she said. "He seemed honest enough. He told me they were just friends."

"Doesn't look like it," Steve replied.

"Why didn't John tell me the truth?" Victoria said, more to herself than to Steve. Then she turned to him suddenly. "You surely don't still think the motive was robbery, do you?"

"We haven't located the war vet yet, who might give us a better idea of that angle," he replied, "but investigating John Gardner too would be worthwhile, I think."

"I'll speak to him again on Monday. You should also look into the whole Megan Jenkins saga." Victoria frowned. "There is something strange about the family."

"Sure, I'll try to fit them in on Monday," Steve said.

She frowned at him, and the thought flitted across her mind that he hadn't tried very hard to find the homeless war vet. Why hadn't he shown interest in pursuing the Jenkins angle? Why hadn't he done more to find the truth? Was there a reason it was too painful for him to pursue? Or was it—

"Did you print out the phone records?" she said suddenly. "I'd like a copy."

"Sure. Remind me when I'm at the office. I'd email them to you, but the file is so big it takes forever to open."

He glanced down at her, holding her gaze for a moment in a way that made her forget what she had wanted to say next.

"I agreed I'd meet Janet," she said and, aware that even to her own ears she was babbling, added, "She invited me to dinner. Where did I put my keys? I am sure they were—" She lifted her handbag, trying to see if they had slipped out onto the couch below. Then she felt a hand over hers and Steve was passing her the keys.

"They fell on the floor," he said, still holding her hand lightly.

For a moment, she thought he was going to kiss her and felt a crazy desire to respond.

"Janet will be waiting for me," she stuttered, standing.

And then his mouth met hers, but so fleetingly that she almost wondered if it had been her imagination.

She instinctively placed her hand on his shirt to ward him off. Instead of releasing her, he slowly drew her closer, and she felt herself melting against the tautness of his chest.

The doorbell rang loudly, and Victoria sprang away.

"Anyone home?" a loud voice called.

"Janet, hi," Steve said, pulling open the door and lifting his eyebrows in resignation.

Janet stepped in, her eyebrows lifting too as she saw the damp towel hanging over the couch.

"Not interrupting you, I hope?" she said. "I got tired of waiting, Victoria, so I thought I'd come meet you."

Victoria glanced at her phone. "Is that the time?" she exclaimed. "I had no idea. We were— that is, we were—"

Janet grinned. "Tell me later."

CHAPTER 12

"Hey, I thought I was coming to dinner," Victoria protested as Janet headed back toward the Hancock Inn. "Where are we going?"

"You are," Janet said. "But first we're going to pick up your stuff from the inn and check you out. Then you're fetching your car from your mother's house, and you're coming to stay with me. Blake and the kids are away camping, which I hate, and I could do with the company."

"Hey, no!" Victoria exclaimed. "I could be here for several weeks still. Longer."

"Detectives must be paid really nicely if they can afford to put themselves up in hotels for weeks at a time," Janet said. "Had you thought about that?"

Victoria grimaced. "I guess not," she admitted. "Maybe I should consider staying with someone I know."

"Where were you thinking?" asked Janet. She grinned. "At the moment, if you don't take me up on my offer, I'd say you'd have to choose between moving in with your mom again and sharing a place with Steve."

"Don't be ridiculous." Victoria blushed.

"True, that is ridiculous," Janet said. "You'd never get on with your mom."

"Cut it out, Janet. Steve and I are colleagues."

"Is that all?"

Victoria stared out the window as they reached a stop street. In the late afternoon sun, a mockingbird swooped down from the sky into a black cherry tree and rose soon after, fruit dripping from its beak.

"Vicky?" Janet prompted. "Talk to me."

Victoria's eyes dropped from the scenery outside to her hands. "I get the feeling he might be interested in more."

"And you?"

"I don't know. Something's holding me back. I'm not ready, I think. Maybe that's it. When I'm with him, my brain turns to mush, but when I gain perspective again, I know it's crazy. During the time he was in Hancock while I was a teen, having him as a friend kind of kept me together. And somehow, I felt protected when Becky and I were hanging out with him."

"From your dad?" Janet asked.

Victoria nodded. "I was terrified he'd come back after the divorce. He'd run away before the police could investigate further and then got himself killed in that freak accident." She buried her face in her hands. "I was so relieved when he died," she muttered. "Is that terrible?"

Janet glanced at her. "No, not at all," she replied. She turned into a driveway. "Here we are," she said. "And by the way, in case you're wondering, neither your mom nor Steve is an option right now. You're staying with me."

* * *

At twilight, the beggar shuffled down the road, a heavy bag over his shoulder, one hand fingering the piece of paper in his pocket. Although his gait was like that of an old man, when he sat by the roadside to lay down his bag and lift up his shoulders, his face was much younger. He might have been in his mid-forties, with shifting, slightly vague eyes, and a mouth that twitched when he was nervous. It was getting late, and he wasn't too sure where he was going. He pulled a bottle out of his bag and unscrewed the lid with fumbling fingers.

"Enough, Todd, enough," he muttered to himself, pushing the brandy back into the bag. He was trying to stop, but the thought made his hands tremble. The bottle neck was still sticking out of the worn plastic shoulder-bag. Something was keeping it from being tucked neatly away. He peered inside. Some soft material was pooled at the bottom of the bag. He tugged at it and got a shock as the multicolored scarf wove its rainbow pattern over his fingers. Quickly glancing left and right to check no one had seen him, he shoved it back into his bag as far as it could go.

"Forgot I had that scarf," he muttered to himself, shaking his head at the brandy bottle. The last couple of nights hadn't been that clear in his mind. And the couple before that too. Ever since . . . With fingers shaking more than ever, he reached for the bottle again and drank until his nerves steadied. A thin rivulet of brandy ran from the corner of his mouth. All of a sudden, he got up, took out the crumpled paper he'd been carrying in his pocket, and held it close to his nose.

His eyes were not that strong, and he had trouble sometimes making out faces in the dark, but there was just enough light for him to read the address on it.

"Hancock Inn," he muttered. "Main Street."

Not far to go. He shrugged his bag onto his back and headed up the road.

CHAPTER 13

Monday morning saw Steve up at dawn. He smiled, a somewhat humorless and enigmatic smile, as he pulled on his work clothes over his lean frame. He paused to grab an apple from the fruit bowl, then hurried out the door, heading for John Gardner's veterinary practice.

"Hey, Claire," he greeted the receptionist, recognizing Karen Timms's daughter. She blushed and found herself tongue-tied but lifted a hand in greeting. "Is John here?"

"Dr Gardner?" she asked. "Yes, but he's busy at the moment, operating. Would you rather see his partner?"

"No, it's Dr Gardner I have to see." He flashed her a smile that would leave her daydreaming for the rest of Monday. "Is it through here?"

"Yes, but—" The gentle brunette rose and placed a hand on the door. "You can't go through there now, Steve — I mean, Detective McCade."

"Steve is good enough for me," he replied. "And this won't wait, I'm afraid."

He hurried through the double doors and to the room on the right, where John was operating.

As the swing-door opened, John glanced up from where he was bent over the operating table. He straightened immediately and rounded the table. A small dog lay unconscious there, beside what looked like bloodied cotton balls.

"Get out," John said, his eyes holding those of Steve.

"Or what?" Steve replied. "You'll deck me again like you did the other day?"

"I'm busy," John said. "Otherwise, yeah, I probably would."

The two men, equally tall and of similar build, watched each other closely.

"You told Detective Wharton you and Rebecca were only friends," Steve said, his voice taut.

"Detective W—? Oh, Victoria." John nodded to himself. "I didn't realize you were on such formal terms." Steve gritted his teeth. John stripped off his surgical gloves. "And what I told her about her sister happens to be the truth."

Steve laughed derisively at that and glanced at the sleeping dog. "Good to see you're not squeamish. What are you doing to that poor mutt?"

"Cleaning his teeth," John replied. "It's a bloody job, especially when they're in such bad shape."

Steve slammed his hand onto the operating table, stirring the dog slightly so that it whimpered. "Let me tell you something, Gardner," he said. "It is you who will end up in bad shape if you don't come clean. What do you know about what happened to Rebecca Wharton? I suggest you tell me. Because she is dead, and if you know something, you need to spit it out. Otherwise, whoever killed her might just decide to come after you, and you wouldn't look nearly as good as that dog if you were lying covered in blood on a steel table."

John was silent.

Something in Steve snapped, and he rammed John up against the wall, his face inches from his.

"What's it to you, McCade?" John panted, straining his muscles to break free. He wrenched himself away and sent Steve hurtling backwards. His back crashed into the operating table just as Victoria and Claire burst in, followed by St. Patrick, who growled menacingly at Steve.

"What do you think you are doing?" Victoria shouted, stepping between the two men. "We can hear you from the waiting room! No, get back!"

Steve shook off her hand, his chest heaving. "I'm going, but I'm not finished with you, Gardner," he said. He turned to Victoria. "You ask this guy about his relationship with your sister and see if you still think he is genuine."

CHAPTER 14

"What was going on this morning?" Karen Timms demanded when she saw Victoria at the police station. "Claire said Steve and John were fighting."

Victoria sat down on the chair opposite Karen and shook her head in disgust. "Don't ask me," she replied. "Steve and I agreed that I would talk to John this morning. He was supposed to be working on the Jenkins angle. Instead, when I got there, I found John Gardner shoving Steve around and the two of them about to go for each other's throats. Afterwards, John had to rush off to an emergency, and I never got to talk to him."

"Apparently John went for Steve the other day too," said Karen. "Steve almost had his nose broken, and John ended up getting stitches. You've seen his scar."

"Steve did that?"

Karen nodded.

"Could John have been harassing my sister?"

"No!"

A bitter laugh sounded at the door, and the women turned to see young Gavin Jenkins, the teenage son of Megan, standing at the doorway.

"You want to know the truth?" he asked, "You want to know what really happened that day John got that scar? Because I saw it."

He ran a hand through his greasy hair and pushed his fringe from his eyes self-importantly.

"They were fighting because John thought Detective McCade was someone else and he was trying to protect Rebecca."

"What do you mean? Who did he think he was?" asked Karen.

"My honorable father," he replied.

Karen blinked. "Your *father*?"

"Come sit down and tell us," Victoria ordered. "I'm getting a crick in my neck staring up at you like this."

Gavin sat down, reveling in his self-importance. "See, my dad is middle-aged," he said. He pulled a piece of gum out of his pocket and shoved it in his mouth. "And he has everything he ever wanted. Big property, good little wife, money, you name it. His son is a bit of a disappointment," he added with a sneer, "but other than that, life has been good for the old man." He shook his head. "And then his mom-in-law, my grandmother, gets sick and winds up in hospital, and he suddenly realizes he may not be immortal."

He blew a bubble and waited until it popped before continuing. "I don't know what garbage they told you about her. The truth is that she needed an operation and was too damn scared, so she kept insisting on doing other stuff than what the doctors said."

"And ended up with gangrene?"

He shuddered. "Yeah."

He was silent while he blew another bubble.

"No one should die like she did." He grimaced. "But it was her own fault. She was stupid. Just like my dad."

"What was your dad stupid about?" asked Victoria. She made eye contact with him to try to keep him focused.

"What about?" he laughed. "About your sister, of course. Darling little Rebecca."

"Don't talk about my sister like that," Victoria snapped, and he smiled as though he was enjoying her anger.

"Sorry," he said unrepentantly, his jaws still chewing. "Anyway, Rebecca was always there at the hospital in her cute little nurse's uniform, and middle-aged Dad suddenly discovered something — someone — he couldn't have."

He leaned back, putting his hands behind his head. "It was pathetic, disgusting, to watch," he said. "Dad would try anything to get her attention. Flowers. Gifts. Always under the pretext of visiting his mother-in-law. And Mom thought his devotion to Gran was *so touching*. I knew of course. I saw him hurrying out the side door with packages under his arm on the days he went without Mom. I saw him coming out the florist with flowers that we never saw at home. So I followed him to the hospital and discovered his dirty little secret."

"And Rebecca?" asked Karen. "How did she respond?"

"I think she was scared," he said. "I went to visit Gran once on my own and saw Dad trying to get close to her, when he thought they were alone."

"So where does the lawsuit fit into all of this?" demanded Victoria.

"I told Mom what was going on. She didn't take it well," Gavin muttered. "She confronted Dad and told him she was leaving him." He laughed out loud. "I've never seen him so frightened. He claimed it was all the nurse's fault. That Rebecca had been after him, harassing him all the time, neglecting my gran. Mom believed him. Wanted to believe him. So when Gran died, he egged her on to file a lawsuit against the hospital. There wasn't really enough evidence to put anything specifically on Rebecca, so they just went generally for the hospital, but Rebecca was implicated. If the hospital lost, she could have ended up without a job."

Victoria glared. "And your father was happy to encourage this lawsuit?"

"Of course. It redirected Mom's anger toward a guilty party she could cope with. If Mom divorced him, he could lose one hell of a lot. His money. His status. Maybe even his home. One pretty little nurse wasn't worth that."

Victoria gritted her teeth, reminding herself that she could not hit him. "And so he left my sister alone?"

Gavin grinned, removing the gum from his mouth to pick his teeth. "You don't know my father, do you?" he said. "He didn't give up. Just became better at hiding what he was doing. He found out where she lived, which is not that difficult when you live in Hancock."

"How do you know all this?" demanded Karen, giving him a dirty look.

"Me? I tracked him," said Gavin with a wave of his hand. "I downloaded an app onto his phone. The same one they downloaded onto mine when I was younger. I didn't even need to leave the house. And then when I saw where he kept going, I went there myself one evening, and it was where I suspected — the home of Rebecca Wharton."

"Why would your father persist in pursuing a relationship that my sister clearly didn't want?" asked Victoria.

He shrugged. "He's a powerful man. He's never heard the word 'no' before, or if he has, he's seen it as a challenge. When he wants something, he goes for it. Doesn't matter who gets hurt."

"But what does this have to do with John and Steve?"

"Right. Sorry, I got sidetracked." He returned the gum to his mouth, and blew another bubble, taking his time and enjoying the impatient irritation of his watchers. "So I went down to the nurse's house again about a week later to see if I could catch Dad out. He didn't have his phone with him, so I wasn't sure where he was. Turns out he wasn't there that night, but John was. And so was Steve. Steve was hammering on Rebecca's door and kept knocking. It was dark outside, and John was inside. John opened the door and shouted at Steve to go away. It sounded like he mistook him for my dad in the dark and then he punched him. Almost knocked him out before he'd realized his mistake, and by that time, Steve was so angry he was ready to kill John too."

"You realize that what you've told us incriminates your father," Victoria said. "He could have become violent when Rebecca kept refusing him."

"Or my mother did." Gavin shrugged. "Had a fit of jealous rage. Either of them could have lost it actually." He leaned back, blew another large bubble, then sat up, smiling, and looked at the two women.

"So," he said. "What do you think? Which one of my parents killed Rebecca Wharton?"

CHAPTER 15

Victoria just needed to get away. No working after hours today. She headed to the Hancock Inn at 5 p.m. and sank down onto a chair outside on the patio, under the shade of an old tree overlooking the lawns. The tranquility and quietness of the greenery helped slow the adrenaline that had been keeping her going over the past while.

Her phone rang, and she answered, her pulse racing. "Steve. Hi."

"Hey, where are you?"

She told him and rang off.

When the server returned a little later with the cocktail Victoria had ordered, the girl suddenly said, "Hey, weren't you staying here?"

Victoria smiled. "For a few days."

"Wait a minute . . . A guy left this for you."

Victoria took the note warily. The paper was folded and dirtied as though it had been carried around for some time.

"Vicky," a voice called, and she glanced up quickly and down again to hide the flush that was spreading from her neck up to her cheeks.

"Steve," she replied casually, turning the note in her fingers.

"What's that?" he asked.

She opened it, frowning. For a moment, she sat still, absorbing the crude message in front of her, then shoved it across the table to him.

The letters had been cut out of a newspaper and sprawled across the battered page, a mixture of upper and lower case: *LeAVE nOw If yOu DoNT wanT to DiE liKE yr SISteR.*

Steve stared at her intently. "Where did this come from?"

"The server said a man brought it," Victoria replied numbly, watching in detached fashion as Steve called the girl over, the threatening words echoing themselves in her head.

"An old beggar brought it," the waitress said, in response to Steve's question. "I quite often see him around."

"The war vet," muttered Steve. "He's finally turned up." He turned to Victoria and placed a hand on her arm. His fingers felt warm and strong. Comforting but at the same time, uncomfortably strong. Confused about how she felt, she withdrew, but only after she had allowed his hand to rest on her arm for a moment.

"You okay?"

"Yeah. I guess." She felt dazed and sick but didn't want to show it.

He frowned. "Whoever wrote this was serious," he said.

She lowered her head into her hands, trying to process the threat. Hancock was so small that everyone living here probably knew she had been staying at the inn, though it seemed unlikely that a wanderer like the war vet would have. Someone must have given him the note.

Someone wanted her gone. Someone was trying to scare her. But who?

Out of the blue, sickeningly, a flashback from her high school days rose up in her mind. She saw a scrawny, pimply teenager from her past, gawky and awkward, with an intense stare that set her skin crawling as he watched her sister across the classroom.

"Whatever happened to Joe Evans?" she exclaimed to Steve suddenly.

She could tell from Steve's reaction that he immediately recalled who she was referring to.

"Became an academic," he said. "Went to some major university and got a PhD."

"So he's no longer in Hancock?" Victoria didn't know whether to be disappointed or relieved.

"Actually, he's back." Steve nodded, his eyes narrowing as he followed her train of thought. "He's doing research on the environment or something. I never see him without wishing I'd beaten him to a pulp."

"For frightening Becky? You pretty well did beat him to a pulp. Don't you remember? You were shouting 'I'm gonna kill you,' and you hit him so hard his nose wouldn't stop bleeding. Have you spoken to him about my sister's murder? Interviewed him?"

"No reason. There's nothing to link him to the case."

"What about his history with my sister? The way he always used to follow her around, trying to carry her bags?" Victoria stood up. "I'm going to track him down and find out if he's involved."

Steve rose too. "Do you want me to come for some protection?" he asked. He was close to her, breathlessly close, and she recalled the brief kiss of the other day.

"Stop it," she muttered to herself, putting herself on the other side of her chair to maintain her distance from him.

"Pardon?" said Steve, startled. A spark lit his eyes in a disturbing way, and she couldn't figure out if it was anger or the intensity of the moment that made him look that way.

"Talking to myself," she said, embarrassed. "A bad habit I've got into from living alone."

At this, Steve laughed, and the enigmatic light vanished from his eyes. "Maybe you need more company?" he suggested.

"Perhaps," she replied. "But not for my meeting with Joe. I'll be fine on my own."

Steve looked at her dubiously, and she tried to laugh.

"I'll be fine," she insisted.

CHAPTER 16

Janet dumped their dirty dinner plates in the sink. "Why would you want to see Joe Evans?"

"Why don't you have a dishwasher?" demanded Victoria. She rolled up her sleeves. "No, let me do it, Janet."

"I'm not going to argue with a woman determined to clean my house. Heaven knows it's in permanent need of tidying," Janet said, putting her feet up on the kitchen table. The room was as cozily cluttered as the rest of her rambling home, which had once been a farmhouse. Victoria searched the cluttered counters for something with which to dry the dishes and eventually discovered a towel draped over the door handle. The only things in the kitchen that didn't need sorting or cleaning were the large framed photos on the kitchen table, one showing Janet's wedding and another with her two children chasing their parents around the garden. Victoria had expected to feel on edge living with someone else after so long living on her own, but whether it was the friendliness of the run-down farmhouse or the warmth of her friend's casual hospitality, she felt oddly at ease.

"The soap is over there," Janet advised. "And you haven't answered my question. What's with the Joe Evans story?"

Victoria scrubbed her plate in the old, rusting sink, then held it up to the light after rinsing, frowning at the plate as if it were a suspect.

"You're washing the dishes, not interrogating them." Janet yawned. "Why Joe?"

Victoria sighed. "Just an off-chance he might be connected," she said. "He was a bit of a stalker in high school."

"Yeah, I know." Janet frowned. "Maybe we were unfair to him though."

"Unfair? What do you mean?"

"I don't know. Just a thought. I was thinking about Joe the other day after we talked about him at the cheese shop. Maybe he wasn't as weird as we thought. On the other hand, what do I know? Maybe he was as creepy as we believed. Go speak to him, and you'll find out."

"I wonder where he is living in Hancock?"

"That's why you needed to move in with your friend." Janet smirked. "Try John Gardner."

"Why him?" Victoria recalled the elusive charm of John's schoolboy smile. Somehow, he didn't seem to be someone who would be spending time with a weirdo like Joe. Then again, what did she know about him really? That however charming he might be, he had got into two fights recently? That he hadn't revealed the full extent of his relationship with her sister?

"I've seen them often on a Wednesday afternoon together at the Harris Center when I go walking with Blake and the kids," she said. "Maybe it's time you went for a stroll?"

After trying several times on Wednesday to get hold of John at his surgery, Victoria decided, more out of frustration than any real hope of seeing either John or Joe, to take out her pent-up energy on a trail.

When she parked at the Harris Center, she considered the same East Side trail where her sister had been found, trying to steel herself to do it. She shut her eyes, hoping to block out the images she kept replaying. Sometimes, she saw Becky already dead when her killer arrived at the Harris Center, about to discard her body as unfeelingly as one would toss away a crumpled cigarette packet. At other times, Becky was still alive, walking through the forest, branches catching on her clothing, delaying her, trying to turn her back from the path she had chosen. Victoria watched her wandering through the woods with — who? She tried to see the face of the murderer, but in her mind's eye, he was always hooded. Victoria's fingers would reach out to rip off the hood, and the image would fade into nothingness. Had the first blow and the shattering of glass been the last sounds her sister had heard, or had she lain alone and dying in the forest? Had she lived to hear the crunching of leaves and jagged breath as her attacker staggered away?

"Not today," Victoria decided eventually, when she could not get her hands to stop shaking. "Steve has been there already."

The Harris Center was fairly busy before Victoria went on her two-mile walk along part of the Thumbs Down trail, but when she returned she found it quieter.

As she neared the Harris Center building, she was greeted like a long-lost friend by a wet-nosed canine.

"St. Patrick!" She smiled and bent down to pat him as she saw John not far behind. She glanced up. "I was hoping I'd see you here."

Victoria thought she saw a slight color touching John's cheeks.

"I mean," she hastily explained, "I need information from you."

His flush faded away. "What information?"

"I'm looking for someone I was at school with. Joe Evans?" Victoria couldn't keep the scorn from her voice as she said his name. "My friend Janet said she'd often seen the two of you together here."

"That's right."

"And?"

"We've been working together helping the Center on a couple of research projects."

"Right. I'm keen to speak to him."

She saw John note her impatience, and a twinkle showed in his eye.

"We've taken on a few projects together, ones that interest me as a vet. Like why Tolman Pond draws huge numbers of ring-necked ducks and other ponds don't."

It was like getting blood out of a stone. Why did he always seem to hold back on her?

"I'm not interested in why you've been hanging out with Joe," Victoria snapped. "Or in your ring-tailed ducks. I want to know where he is."

John grinned. "Ring-necked. Not ring-tailed. And he's in the pollinator garden, which used to be the old swimming pool. Go gently with him."

"I beg your pardon?"

John looked steadily at her, the amusement gone. "He's not one to talk much, but one or two stories of high school have slipped out."

It was Victoria's turn to blush. "What do you mean? He was a real creep when we were at school."

"At least he didn't attack other people, like you egged on McCade to do. That much he told me. He could hardly avoid doing so when he has the scars to show for it."

"He was harassing my sister."

John looked at her skeptically, and Victoria felt a twinge of doubt. Had Joe really been that bad? Had she overreacted in a fit of adolescent self-absorption? Or was he the creep she had assumed?

"Your ring-necked ducks are probably waiting for you," she said. "Don't let me keep you."

John grinned and tightened his grip on St. Patrick's leash. "I only need to worry about the ducks in the fall, but yeah, I'd better get going."

Victoria had not expected him to leave, in spite of her coldness, and a stirring of something that was not pure chagrin but not quite disappointment (or at least, not that she acknowledged) made her say, "You're going already?"

"I'll walk you to the pollinator garden," he said, as though making a concession, but the twinkle in his eyes was back. "I guess the garden was created after you left Hancock so you don't know about it?"

Victoria was too annoyed to reply but looked in the direction he was gesturing. Where the old swimming pool had once been was now a blaze of blooms. The colors were drawing a fluttering and a buzzing of butterflies and bees among anemone-shaped flowers of gold and indigo, and masses of closely clustered orange butterfly flowers. Competing for attention were the purples and pinks of creeping thymes, blazing stars and coneflowers with petals turned downwards like umbrellas.

"There's been a major drop in pollinators," John continued, as though he hadn't noticed her silence, "so a bunch of us got together as volunteers to create an environment where beetles and bees can thrive. And of course, it attracts visitors."

"It's not just for researchers and obnoxious veterinary surgeons then?" asked Victoria, interested despite her irritation.

John laughed. "It's a teaching garden to raise awareness about pollinators and research has been done here too. But it's for everyone. My mom and dad often walk through the garden or relax on one of the benches and watch the birds. Everyone is welcome. Families, elderly couples, hikers, overworked detectives . . ."

She scanned the gardens ahead of them for any sign of Joe as she remembered him.

"He's over there."

Victoria didn't recognize him at first, though the curly dark hair and thick black glasses were still the same. He was bending over a plant, a reed-thin, intense figure. Every now and then his head twitched as though he were speaking to the plants. The serenity of the garden flora was a fitting, maybe even necessary, setting to counteract his nervous energy. Somehow, Joe seemed to belong there. He didn't notice Victoria initially.

"John," he called, pushing his glasses up his nose and jerking his head slightly as he saw that his friend was accompanied.

"Qu-quite impressive display of color," he said, getting the words out with a little difficulty. Victoria had forgotten his stammer. "Very different from when we first started planning the garden. And see h-how far it has come now. Look at the reds and yellows of this *Aquilegia canadensis*. The bees love it by day, and the hawk moths love it after sunset." He stooped to touch the flowers briefly.

"Joe's talking about what most folks call the columbine," said John, nodding at the brightly hued flowers. "Joe, you remember Victoria Wharton? She'd like to talk to you about her sister's death. I must be on my way."

Joe straightened so fast he almost lost his balance. "V-Victoria?" He wiped his hands several times on his baggy jeans, staring at her nervously. "I was so s-sorry about your sister."

"Thank you."

He sat down on a bench nearby and gestured awkwardly to her to sit. Victoria lifted her hand in perfunctory farewell as John departed and sat beside Joe, feeling uncomfortable and out of place to be talking of murder among so much color and life.

"Did you have much to do with my sister?" she asked bluntly.

He shook his head. "Saw her occasionally," he said. "Just to greet though. I never chatted much."

"Why was that?" Victoria was curious. "You always liked her."

The young man jerked his head and took a breath as though preparing himself to speak.

"Th-this is difficult for me to say, you understand," he said under his breath, his eyes dropping to his hands, which were twisting anxiously.

Victoria leaned forward. "What is it?" she demanded, her heart beating faster. "Why didn't you pursue your friendship? She was always kind to you."

Joe nodded and looked up, and she was startled at the tears in his eyes. He paused for a moment, and when he spoke, the words tumbled out, one after the other, in a torrent. "I always had a crush on your sister. Y-you know that. At school—" He interlocked his hands behind his head — "she was the only one wh-who treated me well."

"I'm sorry." It came out as an apology, and Victoria realized it probably was.

"I-I couldn't talk easily, and I struggled with anxiety as a teenager. Although Rebecca was friendly, I was too shy to say much back. I-I used to follow her around." He laughed humorlessly. "Trying to work up the courage to ask her out. Can you believe it? Imagining th-that someone like her would be seen with someone like me? I-I only freaked her out."

"Yeah," conceded Victoria, "you did."

"I was seeing a therapist who encouraged me to s-stand up for myself, and so I tried." He sighed and laughed self-deprecatingly. "It came out all wrong. I never meant to frighten her."

Victoria wanted to swallow but couldn't. Joe's fingers traveled subconsciously to a small place above the hairline where no hair grew, gingerly touching the old wound there.

"Steve?" she asked, her throat dry.

He nodded. "I promised myself to stop b-bothering Rebecca. For good. And I s-stuck to that. I realized then how — off — my behavior must have seemed. How everyone must have been laughing at me. That the things I did appeared weird." His head jerked a little, and he smiled. "Like this. I — can't help it."

"I know," Victoria said. "I do know that now."

"When I graduated high school, I s-swore I would never come back. Went to Princeton and got my doctorate in zoology."

"What made you change your mind?"

He shrugged and looked a little self-conscious. "Time brings perspective, I guess. Y-you see life differently in your twenties compared to your teens. And there is so much research to be done here."

"Ring-tailed ducks," said Victoria. "I know."

"Ring-*necked*," he corrected her with a flash of a smile that disappeared as quickly as it had come. "I— thought maybe if I could come back, make a contribution to Hancock, maybe I c-could make a difference and also prove to myself that I wasn't such a loser as everyone thought I was."

"I think I was the loser," Victoria muttered. "It's going to take me a long time to forgive myself for what you've told me today."

She looked up as she spoke and, recognizing Claire and Karen Timms in the distance, waved to them. Joe followed her gaze and hastily looked down, but she saw his ears turning pink.

"Hey, Joe!" called Claire, waving cheerfully. He muttered a greeting that even Victoria could barely hear and lifted his hand in an abrupt wave.

She looked at him, raising her eyebrows. "Is research the only reason you decided to stay?"

The color of his ears darkened to the rich pink-purple of the coneflower beside him.

"What about you?" he asked, changing the subject. "Are you back to stay?"

Victoria's mind flitted to Steve and then to John, and she frowned. "No, that is, I don't know. At least for now until I discover who killed my sister."

"Have you been on the trail where it happened?"

"No." Victoria shuddered. "Steve has been, obviously. We are working together."

He pursed his lips, and she interrupted the silence. "Were you here when Paula Gardner discovered my sister's body? When the police arrived?"

He nodded.

"You didn't notice anyone in particular?"

"I saw quite a few people," he said, his brow furrowed, "b-but no one stood out."

"You didn't see a beggar?"

"Not that day."

"You've seen him before though?"

"There's a g-guy who has been wandering about in this area for a while. A war vet. P-pretty harmless."

"Maybe not," Victoria said, showing him a photo on her phone of the warning note she'd received. She explained briefly how she had got it. "I assume he was just delivering it for someone else, although I could be wrong."

Joe took the phone and peered closely at the letters. "D-definitely not the handiwork of Todd, the guy I've seen around. We g-got him to do some weeding here in the garden, and I-I chatted a bit with him."

"You sure?"

Joe made a motion with his hand as though he were holding a bottle and tipped it toward his lips. "*Delirium tremens*," he said. "N-no way he would manage all that cutting and pasting of letters with such shaky hands. H-he might know something though. I saw him once or twice in town. Talking t-to your sister."

"I'll follow it up. And nothing else that caught your attention when my sister's body was found?"

He shook his head, and Victoria rose. "Here's my number. Give me a call if you remember. Any time, day or night."

He smiled shyly. "I-I don't sleep easily, so I might just do that."

"You don't sleep well at night?" Victoria sighed, thinking of the nightmares that had started plaguing her again. "That makes two of us."

"Y-you think you will find the person who did it?" said Joe, verbalizing the question she'd been asking herself.

Victoria thought of the warning note she'd received.

She set her jaw. "Yes. Either that, or I'll die trying."

CHAPTER 17

Janet looked over from the driver's seat. "You're going to the concert, like it or not!"

"You are essentially kidnapping me, you realize that?" Victoria replied. She buckled herself into her car seat. "The only reason I'm not resisting is that you have central locking and I can't get out."

"Good. Let's go." Janet dumped a picnic basket on her friend's lap and reversed out of her gravel driveway. "You need to relax," she added. "I've always loved the bandstand concerts on the common."

When they arrived, there was already a small crowd gathering on the common where the bandstand stood, white against the sky. Some families were putting up chairs on the green and taking sandwiches out of picnic hampers, and desserts were being sold to the hungrier members of the audience. Scanning the faces to find Steve, Victoria was disappointed to see only their colleague and her daughter.

"Victoria!" called Claire Timms, coming across to say hello. "We keep meeting! First the vet, then the Harris Center."

"I was interviewing Joe Evans." Victoria smiled. "He knew Rebecca at school."

"Oh, right. Yes, he's really into his plants and animals," said Claire. She smiled shyly back. "The last time I tried to make conversation with him, he spent ten minutes telling me about the ducks on Tolman Pond. Did you come with your mother?"

"What? Is she here?" The news wiped the smile off Victoria's face. She looked around for her mother. Finally, she spotted her in the distance, being helped into her wheelchair from the passenger seat of a green Chevrolet. The woman helping Vera was someone Victoria recognized as a family acquaintance who sometimes gave lifts to her mother on her bad days when driving herself was difficult. Reluctantly, Victoria went over to where her mother was positioned, in the best spot for seeing the musicians getting ready on the bandstand.

"I'm glad you're well enough to be going out," said Victoria stiffly.

"Not really." Her mother's dry voice grated on Victoria's nerves. "Sybil here insisted on bringing me. I'm not up to driving at the moment after the stress of the memorial. I don't know how I will manage with shopping when she goes on holiday next week."

In the expectant pause that followed, she raised her eyes to Victoria's face. Her daughter swallowed. "I'll come by and take you."

"If it won't put you out," her mother replied in that curiously dull monotone, bending her head over to hide the small victorious smile that creased her sunken cheeks. She glanced at Sybil. "Becky always helped so *willingly* with everything."

Sybil murmured something appropriate while glancing apologetically at Victoria.

"My two daughters were always very different," Vera continued. "Becky was of course much better known in Hancock. Everyone would stop us to chat when we went out, right down to that beggar over there."

"What beggar?" Victoria swung around in the direction of her mother's pointing finger, viewing a slightly hunched figure in an old brown raincoat with a bag slung over his shoulder. "The war vet. Todd!" she exclaimed under her breath, starting to run.

"Hey, hey, are you catching a train?" Steve caught her by the arms just in time to stop him running into him full tilt.

"Steve, I didn't know you were here!" she said breathlessly. "The war vet — he's over there!"

She pulled free and ran in the direction of the man. He had taken the bag off his shoulder and was rummaging in it as she raced toward him.

"Todd. Todd!" she shouted, Steve on her heels.

The man glanced up, narrowing his eyes in the twilight in his effort to see who was yelling.

"Are you Todd?" The beggar nodded apprehensively, clutching his bag to his chest.

"Hancock Police," Steve said. "We have a few questions we want to ask you."

"About?" Todd blinked at them over his bag.

"My sister," said Victoria, passing him a photograph of Becky from her wallet.

He held it very close to his face to look, his eyes narrowing in his effort to see more clearly. He started and, looking nauseous, quickly shoved back the photo as though it had burned him. "Yes?"

"We are investigating the circumstances surrounding the murder of Rebecca Wharton. And also the delivery of a threatening note to the Hancock Inn."

Todd glanced from Steve to Victoria with scared eyes, then fumbled in his bag. "I don't know about any murder," he muttered, half to himself, peering up at Steve with large, frightened eyes, then sliding his eyes down again. He emptied out his bag and grasped hold of his bottle with shaking hands and drank, sighing with relief.

"What about the note for Victoria handed in at the Hancock Inn?" demanded Steve.

Todd swallowed and drank again.

"What note?" he said, and Victoria got the impression he was trying to buy time.

"You know nothing about a message, composed of cut-out letters from a newspaper, that told Victoria to leave Hancock?" asked Steve.

"Why would I?" Todd countered, stuffing the bottle back into his bag, along with the other bits and pieces that had fallen out. Victoria held out a scarf to him that had slipped onto the grass and then paused, staring at it intently.

"Where did you get this?" she demanded.

"I don't remember." He reached out to take it.

She snatched it back. "That scarf was my sister's," Victoria said. "I gave it to her when we were still at school. Do you remember, Steve? She loved the rainbow of colors."

Todd suddenly dropped his bag and took to his heels. He was surprisingly agile for someone who appeared so slow and vague, but he was no match for Steve. The young detective sprinted after the beggar and tackled him, bringing him crashing onto his hands.

Victoria hurried after them and caught up. "Come with us," she said grimly.

Steve hauled Todd up and gripped his arm. Todd flailed desperately but to no avail.

Steve smiled triumphantly at Victoria. "We may just have found our killer."

CHAPTER 18

The next morning, Victoria stirred before sunrise. She lay half-awake, her first thoughts flitting automatically to a teenage Becky pirouetting before the mirror in her scarf, her slender fingers extended as she spun.

What happened, Becky? How did a homeless beggar get hold of the scarf you cared about so much? Surely he isn't a killer? Did he steal it from you? Snatch it from your corpse? Did he even realize you were dead? An image of Todd's hands, unsteady and grimy, rose before Victoria's eyes, and she pictured the swollen knuckles and dirt-encrusted nails of his outstretched fingers reaching out to take the cherished garment from her sister's cold, dead neck.

She started as she heard clattering from the kitchen and the crash of a metal lid banging down onto a pot.

"Breakfast," Victoria whispered to herself with relief. Anything to shake the thought of Todd's grasping hands. Getting up, she hurried out of her room and down the passage to the kitchen.

Janet looked up as she came in and passed her a bowl of oatmeal. She waved a hand in the direction of the cutlery drawer. "Help yourself to a spoon. You're off to the police station this morning, I presume? Did you have a good night?"

"I barely slept," Victoria admitted, eating hastily. "I can't believe we might finally have a breakthrough."

"Do you think you will get a confession?"

"Not necessarily of murder, but maybe he can lead us to the person who killed my sister. Last night, we got the server from the Hancock Inn to identify him, and she confirmed he dropped off the note. Steve and I will be questioning him at the station."

A few minutes later, Victoria had dumped the empty bowl into the sink and was on her way. At the police station, she found Todd sitting dejectedly on one of the chairs around Steve's desk, his bag still clasped in his hands, and Steve watching over him. The deep lines above Todd's eyebrows were smeared with dirt, as though he had wiped his hand across his forehead. His cheeks were unshaven, and one side of his face was crisscrossed with faint indentations as though he had slept on an uneven surface. A bruise showed on the other cheek through the grizzled stubble, and Victoria frowned.

"Where did you get that?" she asked.

"It happened when I tackled him last night and he fell, right?" answered Steve for the war veteran. Todd cast a quick, scared glance up and nodded.

Victoria looked hard at Steve for a moment, then sat down and turned her gaze to Todd. "I want the truth," she said. "Did you write that note I got at the inn?"

Todd spread his hands before him. They trembled on his lap. "How could I?" he asked, echoing what Joe Evans had said. He sighed. "My hands are not so steady," he added simply.

"Then who wrote the note?" demanded Steve, looming over the beggar.

Todd blinked as though confused and paused. "I was walking outside Hancock," he said, taking the time he needed to remember, for the days often passed in a blur. "It was getting dark, and I was looking for somewhere to sleep for the night. Not too cold, not too far off the road."

He scratched his head in his effort to recall the details. "Someone came up to me and said he would pay me to take a message to the Hancock Inn. Said it was for the sister of Rebecca Wharton." He sighed, his vague eyes watery. "Most people won't give me anything," he said. "Because they think I will just drink if they give money. I keep trying to stop, but sometimes I drink too much."

Victoria, noting the broken veins on his cheeks and the bloodshot eyes, suspected this was an understatement.

"Rebecca was always kind. She didn't give me money—" He shrugged — "but she would buy fruit and keep it with her in her car or bag for when she saw me."

"Who gave you the note?" asked Victoria.

Todd frowned hard and then shook his head from side to side in confusion. "I couldn't see his face. My eyes can't see well in poor light."

"Who do you know in Hancock who might have given you the note?"

"Most people know me," Todd said. "I have done some odd jobs here and there. For the churches in and around Hancock. For some of the bigger houses needing grass cut or gardening done. For the animal doctor."

Victoria glanced, startled, at Steve, who sat suddenly, his eyes riveted to Todd's face. Had the man who had given Todd the note been John?

"What color was the hair of the man who spoke to you? Dark?" demanded Steve. "Red-haired?"

"It might have been," Todd said, blinking as he tried to remember.

"Which?" snapped Steve.

"Either," said Todd. "It was dark, and I don't really remember. I drink sometimes," he repeated, as though this was sufficient explanation — which, Victoria guessed, it probably was.

"Who knew that your eyes were poor?" asked Victoria. "No one you could identify would have risked using you to take the note."

"Oh, everyone." Todd nodded and kept nodding as though rather pleased at last to be able to give a more definite answer.

"Were you on the Harris Center trail when Rebecca was found?" Victoria demanded. "Did you leave a beer bottle there? We are going to have to fingerprint you to check."

Todd looked scared. "It wasn't my bottle," he said, his eyes shifting rapidly. Victoria was sure he was lying.

"What about the scarf you had?" She pointed to his bag. "Where did you get that?"

Todd suddenly shrank into himself. He stared in front of him, his expression blank.

Steve bent forward, his shoulders tense. "Where did you find the scarf? Did you steal it?" When he got no answer, he rose and stood next to the older man, towering over him. "I asked you a question."

Todd thought for a moment, his eyes shifting slowly from Steve to Victoria and then back again. Victoria watched closely as the fear slowly drained from his eyes to be replaced by a curious, sly glance, as though he had suddenly realized something to his advantage.

"The scarf's my secret," he murmured. He took it from his bag and ran the material through his fingers, caressed it. "Its secret is safe with me." Then he lapsed back into silence, his face vacant once more.

Victoria stood up in disgust. "We're not going to get anything more from him today," she said. "Probably Rebecca gave him the scarf without telling my mother."

"Can I go?" asked the beggar, trying to rise. Steve pushed him down again, but Victoria jerked her head at the door. Steve frowned and shook his head, but she spoke before he had a chance to contradict her.

"You can go," Victoria said. "Where can we get hold of you if we have more questions?"

"I'm usually on the common in the late afternoon," replied Todd, shuffling eagerly toward the door. "Or down near the Meeting House. You can meet me there if you have *anything* to ask me."

Again, that disturbingly cunning look crossed his face just for an instant before his usual blank expression returned. The door closed behind him.

"Why did you let him go?" Steve demanded.

Victoria sank back into her seat, exhausted. She closed her eyes. "He wasn't going to tell us any more. I suspect he was on the scene, maybe saw her body and kept quiet. But you surely don't think he did it?"

"Of course I do," Steve replied, and her eyes flew open. "He is wandering around with property belonging to your sister. He probably sold her phone long ago. No doubt he accosted her on her walk — maybe she didn't have any food for him. Maybe he was tired of getting food and in need of money to buy alcohol. So he attacked her and accidentally killed her."

"Why didn't he take her cell phone when he killed her then?" questioned Victoria.

"You've seen the guy. His brain is so addled with alcohol he can hardly think straight, even first thing in the morning. He probably ran off in fright when he went too far and killed her. But later, his need for alcohol overcame his fear. He hid in the undergrowth and watched as Paula discovered the body. Then as soon as she left, he grabbed your sister's phone to sell so he could buy alcohol and her scarf to keep him warm. What do you think?"

Victoria pursed her lips as she considered his arguments.

"No," she said at last. "None of it makes sense. I mean, how likely is it he would have known I was staying at the Hancock Inn or even known who I was? It's not like he is really part of society in Hancock here. He hangs around on the fringes doing bits of work where he can. And who would buy a phone from him round here? Everyone knows about what happened to Becky. He'd have been in jail before he could get anywhere close to buying liquor. We haven't found the phone in his possession, and it hasn't turned up anywhere else. In any case, he hardly strikes me as someone who is violent. He is so wobbly on his legs, my sister would easily have fought back even if he had tried anything. And why would he want to steal her phone when he has been getting cash for jobs here in Hancock?"

Steve stared at her, clenching his jaw as though trying to control his temper. "You don't make allowances for the clouded mind of an alcoholic," he said, trying to keep his voice even. "Maybe you can rationalize away everything with your logic, but alcohol can do weird things to people — make them behave differently from usual. Like my mother." He laughed bitterly. "Maybe even drive him to use more force than we would think him capable of."

"What about the note? He isn't capable of that!"

"The work of Maurice Jenkins?" Steve suggested. "Think of everything you told me about him. Did that ever occur to you? If you keep investigating him, he might end up getting exposed for his harassment of your sister — and attempted adultery."

"All I know is that I can't imagine Todd committing violence," replied Victoria. "I think he knows more than he admits, but he's not a murderer."

"And all I know is that you've just let go our most likely suspect," replied Steve, his voice rising. "I could have got a confession out of him!"

"You mean the same way you got him to cooperate with us this morning?" Victoria asked, a bite to her tone.

"What are you talking about?"

"That mark on his face?"

"He already told you how he got that bruise," Steve said. "He fell. Don't forget, before you accuse me of police brutality, whose side you are on."

Victoria closed her eyes. She heard the door slam. When she opened them again, he was gone. For a moment, she considered going after him, but pride stopped her. Doubt filled her mind as she thought back on what she had said. Had she gone too far?

CHAPTER 19

"I need to get out," Victoria told Janet that evening as they ate dinner together.

"Was my meatloaf that bad?" Janet asked, clearing the dishes from the large wooden kitchen table and dumping them in the sink. "Or are you just trying to shirk the dishwashing?"

"Both," groaned Victoria. She smiled. "It's been a really long day. A really lousy day."

"The interrogation of the war vet didn't go as planned?"

Victoria slumped down in her chair and squeezed her eyes between her thumb and forefinger. "I don't know what to think," she said. "I honestly don't see Todd killing anyone. If he did decide to kill anyone, he'd be so slow, any potential victim would long since have figured out what he intended and have had the opportunity to run away."

"And Steve disagrees?"

Victoria pushed her chair away from the table and stood up, rolling her shoulders to unstiffen her neck.

Janet placed her hand on her hip. "Have you guys been fighting?"

"No, not — yes. Actually, we have. I don't think he's talking to me at the moment. And I'm permanently on edge. This case is driving me crazy." Victoria rubbed her temples.

"Headache?" enquired Janet, and Victoria nodded.

"I usually get pain here," Victoria said, placing her hand on her chest. "It's an anxiety thing, I guess. But now it's diversifying and spreading upwards. My head feels like it's on fire."

"Go for a walk," Janet said. "I'll do the dishes."

"You're sure?"

Janet shooed her toward the back door. "Go on. Go, before I change my mind."

Victoria swung open the stable door and stretched her neck to one side and then to the other, breathing in the coolness of the evening air. She walked down past the Vestry, glancing up at Hancock's Meeting House as the historic bell — Paul Revere's #236 bell — chimed.

"Eight p.m. already," Victoria murmured to herself, checking the bell's time against her phone. She hastened past the cemetery and went on to Norway Pond. One or two families were still swimming when she arrived, and she sat down by the waters. When the swimmers started heading home, she remained where she was, seeing, in her mind's eye, the waters of the pond freeze over, as they did in winter, and her sister skating effortlessly across the ice. She closed her eyes, the memories of Becky slowly erasing the pounding pain in her head. She wasn't sure how long she stayed that way.

When she eventually opened her eyes, the air held a chill, and the light had faded. She gave a slight shiver and sat more upright. She was alone, and suddenly even the innocence of childhood memories couldn't erase the fear of the dark that later memories of her father had brought.

"Home," she said to herself, aware of the bitterness in her voice. It wasn't far to go after all. As she turned, a hooded figure grabbed her from behind and shoved her into the water. She had a split-second in which to scream before the water engulfed her. Spluttering, she came up for air, only to have a merciless hand grip her neck and force her head under again. She fought furiously, and felt the hand loosen momentarily as she jabbed her elbow hard into her assailant's abdomen at the base of the ribcage. For a moment, she thought she could make it out of the water before her attacker recovered, but her foot slipped, and she felt those merciless hands again. They closed around her neck and jerked her close to her assailant. Almost subconsciously, she registered the faint smell of cologne as he breathed in her ear.

"Leave Hancock unless you want to end up in the cemetery."

Victoria struck his chin, and he staggered backwards, swearing. At the same time, she heard barking and saw a welcome sight as St. Patrick, floppy jowls flapping almost ludicrously as he ran, tore toward her. The hooded attacker saw him too, scrambled to his feet, and took to his heels. St. Patrick feinted a rush in his direction, barking viciously, then turned back to Victoria, his tongue hanging out and ears waving as wildly as his jowls. Victoria's legs buckled under her as she realized she was safe, and she sat down, St. Patrick nuzzling her affectionately.

"Who's there?" called a familiar voice through the darkness, and Victoria sat up on her haunches, her arm around the dog.

"John! I'm here. By the pond!"

"Victoria?"

John hurried over to them. "You look like you almost drowned," he exclaimed, pulling her up onto her feet and noting how her sodden shirt stuck to her.

"You mean, like someone almost drowned me?" Victoria replied. "I was attacked."

John looked startled. "Come with me," he said, glancing around. "I don't want to have to rescue you a second time if the guy is still out here."

"It was your dog that rescued me," she pointed out, patting St. Patrick's head. She followed John to a nearby house, a neat square building with a small garden and two cats sitting on the wall.

"Home," he said. "Come in."

The house was brightly lit, and she closed her eyes in relief as she stepped inside. She was vaguely aware of soft-backed chairs of beige and a large photograph of a smiling young woman on the wall.

"You okay?" John asked.

"Yep. Just need to sit for a moment."

"Not in those clothes," he said firmly. "You'll ruin my furniture. Here, go into my room. There are towels in the en suite bathroom, and grab whatever fits to wear. You can tell me what happened once you're dry. Shall I walk you home a bit later, or do you want me to phone someone to come fetch you?"

"Yeah, do you have Janet's number? Thanks."

Victoria came through a few minutes later, wearing an over-long floral dress and wringing water from her hair into a towel.

John swallowed as he saw the dress and turned away.

"This suits me better than it does you," Victoria joked, sitting down. "Do you have a sister?"

She glanced up at the wall again at the smiling young woman and then back to John.

"I was married," he said, sitting down opposite her. "Gina died a few years back. I forgot I still had a few of her things. I thought I'd given them all away when I moved here."

Victoria studied the picture of Gina. She could not have been older than in her early twenties. "She looks as though she had such vitality, as though she was smiling at the entire world."

"She did," John said shortly. Victoria wanted to ask what had happened to her, but he forestalled her.

"Who attacked you?" he asked. "It seems crazy."

Victoria described briefly what had happened.

"I couldn't see him," she finished her story. "He wore a hood, and it was dark. All I could tell was that he was a tall man, possibly your height, I'd say, maybe even taller. When he grabbed me and held me under the water, I thought I'd had it, but I don't think he wanted to kill me. Just scare me."

John whistled. "Who would want to do that in tranquil Hancock?"

She caught his eye and held it for a moment, but before she could answer, she was interrupted by hammering on the window. "Janet already?" exclaimed Victoria.

John pulled open the door and took a step back in surprise as he saw Steve on the doorstep.

"What are you doing here?" he demanded. He folded his arms across his chest.

"Janet was having car trouble, so she phoned me and asked me to walk across and fetch Vicky. She was nervous to walk after hearing about the attack."

Victoria flushed at the sight of Steve, remembering their last meeting.

He strode up to her, frowning, and lifted his hand to touch her neck lightly where she could feel bruising already from the attack. She noticed the way his shirt strained as his muscles contracted beneath it, and she looked away quickly.

"Are you hurt?"

Victoria felt her neck. "Not too bad," she replied awkwardly.

"Any idea who might have done it?" There was a formality in his tone that told Victoria he hadn't forgotten their argument.

"Presumably Becky's murderer?" she replied. "Isn't that logical?"

"Or someone you are investigating who has a secret of their own," offered John.

"How would you know?" Steve said.

John held Steve's gaze silently for a tense moment and then smiled. "I suppose because we all have secrets," he said, more to Victoria than to Steve.

Victoria glanced again at the picture of Gina. "Even you?" she asked.

He followed her gaze and nodded. "Even me."

CHAPTER 20

Claire Timms stared at the deep purple markings on Victoria's throat. "You look like you've been strangled," she exclaimed.

Victoria, who was with her mom doing her shopping at Hancock Market after work, stopped to adjust the scarf that had slipped from her neck. "I just about was," she said ruefully, picking out rhubarb for her mother and passing it to her. "I can barely swallow."

Vera prodded the rhubarb with a judgmental finger.

"These ones are too short," Vera said, passing the crimson rhubarb back to Victoria without bothering to look at her. Victoria put it back, trying not to lose her temper. "Becky always chose longer rhubarb."

"My mom told me you had been attacked," said Claire. "I couldn't believe it. We were at Norway Pond earlier that day."

"Pity your mom wasn't still there when the guy went for me."

A shy cough interrupted them, and Victoria turned to see Joe behind her.

"I overheard you. W-was the attacker the same as y-your sister's killer, do you think?" he asked, his stutter worsening as he saw Claire.

"Surely it must be?" Claire said. She stared at him. "Why even ask that?"

Joe turned the same color as the rhubarb. "Different modus operandi," he suggested. "Rebecca was killed. From what John told me, your assailant had no intention of actually taking your life."

"Won't you get me some honey, Victoria?" her mother interrupted. "Make sure it's not too big." Victoria hurried off to get the honey and brought it to her mother.

She sighed. "Not this small." She dismissed the bottle. "I prefer a bigger size. It lasts longer."

"No problem." Victoria grinned and immediately passed her the bigger bottle that she had been holding in her other hand. For once, Vera was left without a word to say and banged the bottle into the basket on her lap.

"I often walk on my own in the evenings, especially if it is hot," said Claire. "But now I'm too scared."

"You need a friend to walk with you," said Victoria, and when silence followed, she trod on Joe's toe. Joe took a deep breath.

"Several fascinating species of owl come out after dark . . ." he muttered, trailing off at the end of his sentence as he realized he was losing his thread. "That is, I don't know if you— if either of you are interested in them. O-owls, I mean."

"Not particularly," said Claire, looking puzzled as she tried to follow his train of thought.

He flashed Victoria a nervous smile and ploughed on. "I-I rather enjoy watching them myself. If that is, if you feel unsafe in any way, you could let me know . . ." He took another breath.

"Just give me a shout, and I'll hold your hand," a confident voice interrupted him, and Claire looked up to see Steve smiling disarmingly at her.

"Hi." Claire blushed, her big eyes widening, not quite able to believe he was offering her his protection.

"Steve," muttered Victoria awkwardly, glancing at her mother, but Vera didn't even acknowledge him.

"Hey, Victoria," he said as though he had only just noticed her and turned back to Claire. Victoria clenched her hand on the wheelchair handles. Did Steve honestly think such juvenile tactics were going to work? He noticed her tightening hands and grinned. "So just give me a shout if you need me, Claire. You know where I live."

"Thank you," stammered Claire.

"That's m-my cue," said Joe. He smiled a little wistfully at Claire, and something in his face touched her.

"Hey, thanks for the offer, Joe," she said, reaching out her hand to his arm. "I guess working for the vet I should probably brush up on my owls."

"Good career move," agreed Joe hastily, a twinkle lighting his eyes behind the thick glasses, and Claire found herself smiling back. He put up his hands as if to adjust his glasses then lowered them instead to fidget with his phone. "I think I h-have your number. I'll give you a call, Claire. Sometime when you're free. No rush." He raised his hand in his usual jerky way to say goodbye, but Victoria noticed the smallest swagger in his movements and hid a grin at Steve's fury.

"Beaten at your own game, Detective McCade," she murmured, as Claire also headed off to finish her shopping.

"You think so?" he asked, touching her cheek lightly. He was so close to her that the scent of his aftershave clung to her, drawing her closer.

"I'm still waiting for my apology from you," he said, his eyes catching hers, leaving her feeling as though they were the only two in the building. She opened her mouth to reply, and at the same moment, her mother cleared her throat.

"I still haven't got my rhubarb," she complained.

Steve grimaced, and Vera smiled gently at him, her eyes lingering maliciously for a second longer than necessary as she savored his disappointment.

Vera's words brought Victoria back to earth, and she recalled Steve's tactics to try to make her jealous of Claire.

She turned away from him to pick out the rhubarb and straightened.

"Keep waiting," she advised him. She passed the rhubarb to her mother and released the wheelchair brakes so they could go. "See you at the station, Detective McCade."

CHAPTER 21

"Listen, Victoria, I wonder if I could have a word with you privately?"

Victoria, who had been sitting taking a lunch break on the common, put down her sandwich in surprise.

"Hello, Mr Jenkins," she replied. He smiled at her, a calculating smile, intended to charm and placate, she suspected. She watched him warily.

"Call me Maurice."

"Maurice, then. Did you attend the concert the other night?" she asked, nodding toward the bandstand.

"No, no, I was meeting with our lawyer about the hospital case. May I join you?"

"Would you not rather talk to me at the station? I'm on my lunch," said Victoria pointedly.

"This can't wait. And I prefer speaking to you in private. It's a confidential matter." He smiled again, showing carefully whitened teeth. He was a big man, probably Steve's size, Victoria reckoned, but heavier. Although he had a slight paunch when he was relaxing, he would still, to most people, appear an attractive man, a prosperous, middle-aged man. Victoria, though, thought he reminded her of a wolf.

She glanced at her watch. "What is it, Maurice?"

He sidled a little closer, and she immediately stiffened.

"It's about my son," Maurice confided. "I don't quite know how to say this, but Gavin is not well."

Victoria shifted away from Maurice until she could breathe again and looked at him directly. "He seemed fine the other day when I saw him at the police station."

"Police — dammit," Maurice swore softly. "So Megan was right." He glanced quickly at Victoria, and his face assumed a softened expression. "We thought our boy might have done something silly."

He fidgeted with his cuff as though buying time to plot his next move. "Gavin has what is called an inferiority complex," he said. "I was born naturally talented at sport and at academics and was always popular at school. Gavin is none of those things."

"I have no idea about his sporting ability or his popularity, but he seemed pretty sharp to me," Victoria replied.

Maurice gave her a sorrowful grin. "His only talent, I'm afraid, is in telling lies," he said. "At that he is particularly adept."

"Why would he do that?" Victoria demanded.

Maurice shrugged. "Jealousy," he replied. "Simply put, my son is viciously, irremediably jealous of me. He somehow feels that rather than trying to reach the success that I achieved, if he can prevaricate and spread stories about me to his friends, he can boost his self-esteem."

"I assume you're concerned about what he told me and want me to believe it was all lies," said Victoria. "But I'm hardly one of Gavin's friends."

"So he did talk to you about me." Maurice's face darkened. "What did he say?" he demanded, switching off the charm and introducing a menacing note into his voice.

A quiver of fear ran down Victoria's back. She shivered. Something made her feel that Maurice could be dangerous. "What do you think he said?" she countered.

"He told you about Rebecca, didn't he?" snapped Maurice.

"Maybe," Victoria said. "Want to tell me your side of the story?"

Maurice recovered his grip on himself and breathed out slowly. She noticed his hand was a little sweaty as he adjusted his tie. "I'm a one-woman man," he said, twisting the solid platinum ring on his wedding finger. "Megan is my world."

Victoria maintained a cynical silence.

"Being successful, I sometimes attract unwanted attention from other women," he said carefully. "Even much younger women."

Victoria supposed his tone was meant to be one of regret, but to her it sounded more like pride. "That must be difficult for you," she said drily.

"Exactly," he replied, glancing quickly at her.

Victoria pre-empted what was coming next, trying to control her temper. "And when," she asked, "did you first notice that my sister, a beautiful, innocent, dedicated nurse with more than enough male attention from guys her own age, had fallen under your spell?"

"I can understand your disbelief," Maurice said. He gave a little laugh. "I was taken aback myself." He sighed. "I made the mistake of being a gentleman," he said. "I was too courteous when I should have been blunt. I thought I had made myself clear, but your sister clearly mistook my politeness for encouragement."

"And I assume you have proof of her behavior?" asked Victoria. "Phone records perhaps? Like we have for Rebecca?"

Maurice paled for a moment. "She was too clever for that," he said. "She knew her job might be at risk if my wife caught her out. But she wrote me letters, which I burned," he added quickly. "And pestered me continuously when I visited my mother-in-law on my own."

"And you couldn't take your wife along?"

"It wasn't always convenient. Or she sometimes had other commitments."

"Why not just tell Megan then? I imagine most wives would find it fairly easy to shift their own commitments when their husband's commitment was under attack?"

He shook his head. "I should have," he said. "But she was already under so much pressure worrying about her mother that I didn't want to burden her further."

"And then she found out?"

Maurice winced. "That was the worst of it. My son told her. His version of the story. Completely inaccurate and libelous, but that didn't bother him." Genuine anger made his voice unsteady. "I explained repeatedly what had actually happened. I was finally able to convince Megan."

"But Gavin maintains you were to blame?"

"Exactly. It gives him a thrill, the belief that he has power over me, and the ability to bring me down. I took him to the best psychologist around, who confirmed he is untrustworthy. Yet still he tries to hurt me. His own father. All to boost himself and to get attention." He placed his head in his hands. "I don't know what to do," he said.

Victoria looked at him. "Why not just give him the attention he craves?" she suggested.

* * *

Norway Pond. Victoria forced herself to the water's edge. Steve had been there with her, the day after the attack, and possible evidence had been collected by a crime scene investigator, but something had driven her to go back after work today, although she made sure it was well before sunset.

She sat at the water's edge, the skin on the back of her neck prickling as she forced herself to relax and concentrate. Which direction exactly had the attacker come from? The high-pitched call of a tree swallow made her jump to her feet, her throat constricting. *It's just a bird. That's all. Just breathe. In. Out. In. It's light still. You're safe here today. Do you understand? Keep breathing.*

She heard a rustle of leaves, and instinctively, she found herself looking for something to use to defend herself. Sand to throw in the attacker's eyes, a stone she could use as a weapon . . . *Think, Victoria. Don't freeze. Not like you did when you were young. This is not your father.*

She closed her eyes, trying to block out the images that came rushing at her.

"Vicky!"

She heard it again, louder.

"Vicky! It's me."

She heard snuffling and panting and opened her eyes in relief to see John with St. Patrick.

"Quite a coincidence. You seem to appear whenever I'm around here," she said. She swallowed, trying to get rid of the dryness in her mouth and throat.

"Actually, I saw you and followed you down. Or rather, St. Patrick did," amended John, a little awkwardly. "I didn't want a repeat of the other day, so I thought I'd better check on you." He looked at her more closely and his brow contracted. "Come here," he commanded, stretching out his hand to her. She held back, staring at him.

He dropped his hand and went to her.

"I'm going to put my arm around you and help you away from the bank, okay?" he said.

Victoria froze, and he sighed. "You're sweating and pale, and you look like you might faint, Victoria," he explained. "Not a good combination near water."

"Don't touch me. I can do it myself."

John put up his hands and backed off. "I'm not touching you. But come away from the water."

Victoria slowly made her way to drier ground. St. Patrick bounded to her and leaped up, placing his paws on her chest. Her knees gave way unexpectedly, and she sat down with a thud.

"Good dog," John grinned. "He'd make an excellent doctor," he told Victoria. "Knows exactly what to do. And of course, he can't be sued, so he has no problem pushing his patients around."

Victoria shivered although it was warm.

John sat down near her, keeping enough distance so that the St. Bernard could comfortably fit between them.

"What are you doing here?" he asked. "Surely it's not a good idea to come alone?"

"It's pretty safe in the day, I'd say."

"It's safe in the evening for most people too," he reminded her.

Victoria stroked St. Patrick, focusing on the smooth softness of his fur and counting how many times she stroked him. *One, two, three, and breathe. Four, five, six, and breathe. Breathe. Just breathe.* She could feel her heart rate steadying, and her pulse no longer hammered so wildly in her neck.

"I felt I had to come once more, to see if there was anything that would give a hint as to who attacked me."

John shifted and as he did so, felt something hard beneath his fingers. He dug it out of the ground and held it up to the light.

"A cufflink," she said.

"Does that mean anything?" he asked.

"I don't know. It looks vaguely familiar, somehow. I'll keep it anyway."

John didn't comment but looked around. "We often come this way to walk. St. Patrick loves the water. Gina used to love water too. Swam like a pro."

"How long were you married?" Victoria asked.

"Not long enough," he said. He paused then changed the subject. "And you haven't ever been married?"

Victoria shuddered.

"A very comprehensive answer," he grinned. "You think it would be that bad?"

"I'm glad to be single," she replied, pushing the thought of Steve from her mind. "The number of domestic violence incidents I had to intervene in when in Chicago was frightening."

"You don't long for family life?" John asked, and she noticed he looked away as he spoke as though seeing something intangible to anyone else but him.

Victoria laughed shortly. "I've had enough 'family life' to last me a lifetime," she replied. "'Family life' put me in therapy for more years than I want to remember."

John was silent. Then he said hesitantly, "Want to talk about it?"

Victoria spread out her hands on her knees, staring at them. "Not really, although it is an open secret in Hancock," she replied. "My father was abusive. I went to the police, both to protect myself and to prevent him from doing the same to my sister. He ran away to escape arrest shortly after the divorce and died in a freak car accident. I thought I was okay now."

"A traumatic attack like the one you suffered recently could bring it all back again."

Victoria nodded and put her arms around St. Patrick. "My sister's death. Coming back home to Hancock. The attack here at Norway Pond. Major triggers. I struggle to sleep, and when I do, the memories all keep coming back." She put her face against St. Patrick's fur, and he licked her.

"He's a good therapy dog," teased John. "You might not let me take your hand to help you away from the water, but that dog has you wrapped around his claw."

"He's gorgeous," said Victoria. "If I had a dog like this with me at night, I don't think I'd ever have another nightmare." She looked thoughtfully at John. "And you, John? What is your deep, dark secret? You said you also had skeletons in your closet."

John smiled faintly. "Mine?" he asked. "That's easy. I killed my wife."

Victoria scrambled to her feet, her shoes slipping in her hurry. When she saw John wasn't moving, she froze. He wasn't even looking at her. He was staring out across the water, his hand over his mouth.

"Gina was an accountant. We were also living in Chicago at the time. Like you do. She uncovered irregularities in the firm she was working for. She asked me what to do. She just wanted to resign, but I told her to report it to HR, little realizing that those in HR were involved too — they were being paid to keep quiet about the embezzlement. After speaking to HR, she was attacked one night at work and her neck badly bruised. She tried reporting the irregularities again, this time to her boss."

"What happened?" asked Victoria.

"Those who were guilty covered their tracks and made it look like she was the guilty one. She got dragged through an internal investigation and finally was questioned by the police. They searched our home. At the same time, she miscarried our child."

"That's terrible," said Victoria, still poised to run.

"Yeah. I thought she was coping, but the strain was too great."

"Suicide?"

"Aneurysm."

He reached out a hand to pat St. Patrick as though he was soothing the dog and not vice versa.

"Why do you say you killed her?" Victoria asked.

"She was following my advice. If she'd just resigned, she wouldn't have been under so much pressure. Maybe our baby would have survived. Maybe the aneurysm wouldn't have happened. I believe so, anyway. The doctor said perhaps it could have been avoided." He swallowed. "I killed her."

"It could have happened anyway. You know that, right?"

He nodded and turned to look at her with a shrug. "Anyway," he said, "that's it. That's my secret. I live with the knowledge that if I'd protected her better, she might still be alive."

CHAPTER 22

The evening was cool, and Victoria had her feet tucked up on the shabby-chic couch, her sweater pulled over her knees and her cup cradled in her hands.

Janet sipped her tea and looked over at her. "So, the annual Hair Ball Gala is coming up," she said Janet.

"*Hair Ball*? Are you kidding me?"

In reply, Janet held across her phone to Victoria so she could see the online advert for herself. "Don't you remember from when we were kids? It's at the Keene Country Club, and it's to collect money for shelter animals. The theme is Mission: PAWSible. You go dressed as a secret agent."

"Enjoy. Sounds fun." Victoria took a sip of tea.

"I'm not going alone. Blake phoned to say they're only getting back the day after the ball. Apparently they're enjoying themselves and have been adopted by a stray puppy who follows them everywhere. Anyway, long story short, you're coming with me to the ball."

"No way," Victoria said hastily. "You're on your own."

"And if Steve asks you?"

"Don't be ridiculous," Victoria snapped. "Things are tense between us right now."

"What happened?"

"I accused him of hitting Todd, the war vet," Victoria muttered. She explained the story.

"That's insane!" Janet exclaimed. "Why would he do that? From what you told me, Todd is permanently drinking or suffering from withdrawal. He probably fell."

"Maybe," replied Victoria in a small voice. "Actually, that's what Steve says happened."

"There you go," Janet replied. She stared at Victoria hard. "You're deliberately sabotaging any chance with Steve. You know that?" she asked. "Did you see Todd fall at all?"

"Yes," replied Victoria. A sinking feeling spread down through her chest and into her stomach.

"And was it hard enough to cause bruising?

"I guess. Maybe. I don't really remember how he fell."

"So why are you so scared?"

Victoria put down her teacup so she could wrap her arms around her knees. "I keep wondering if I can trust him, you know."

"Victoria, this is Steve we're talking about. You've known him since you were a teenager."

"Yeah, but I wonder if he's withholding something from me. When we first met up after my sister's death, he called her Becky. No one does that except those really close to her."

"The guy knew her! Of course he was close to her!"

"But even so—"

Janet interrupted her. "Okay, then, what about going to the ball with John?"

"Why John?"

"He went out of his way to check up on you yesterday when you went back to Norway Pond. And then he walked you home again. And sat drinking coffee with us for an hour."

"I think he's lonely. He lost his wife a while back."

"So help him feel less lonely!"

"Will you cut it out?" Victoria exclaimed. "I'm not interested! Didn't you hear me say his wife died recently? He's working through her death."

Janet lifted her eyebrows. "He'd obviously worked through enough to fall for your sister."

"That's another reason not to go with him." Victoria lifted her head. "He still hasn't told me what exactly their relationship was. Why would a guy who'd agreed just to be friends call her every day for three weeks? Makes him seem more like a stalker."

"He doesn't strike me as a stalker type."

"I don't know. I just don't think I can—"

"Trust him," interrupted Janet. "I know."

Victoria stared at her friend and groaned, rubbing her hand over her forehead. "I have a problem, don't I?" she said.

"You said it, not me," replied Janet. "But yeah, you do. I don't think you're as uninterested in a relationship as you pretend. I think you're just scared."

"It does frighten me," muttered Victoria.

Her friend tapped her on the arm. "The question is not whether they are trustworthy. It's about you."

"I know." Victoria sighed, feeling suddenly drained. "The question is, will I ever feel ready to take a chance at trusting someone again?"

CHAPTER 23

Victoria was at the police station, the coffee she had poured herself long forgotten, reading through her sister's file again, when she realized something was missing.

"Steve?"

He came through from the next room.

"Don't you ever stop working?" he asked, nodding at her untouched coffee cup.

She ignored the question.

"Where are the phone records?"

"Sorry, I still need to add them to the file. It's been hectic." He spoke slightly dismissively, and she was immediately nettled.

"I want those records," she snapped. "What's been keeping you so busy anyway?"

"Fatal Vision Goggles," he said. He grinned at her blank stare. "It's a program we were doing at ConVal High School. We joined forces with Liquor Enforcement and let the kids do various simulations using goggles that mimic visual impairment and then got them to do sobriety tests. We're looking to extend the program now throughout the community."

He passed her a pair, and she put them on, curious. "These really affect your judgment," she exclaimed, trying to walk in a straight line.

"Yeah," said Steve. He removed the goggles from her head and smiled down at her in a way that made her heart hammer in her chest.

She took a deep breath, trying to muster up her courage. "Right," she muttered, clenching and unclenching her hands, "I hate to admit that I'm wrong, but Janet and I were chatting about the Hair Ball Gala last night and I don't know how, but we got chatting about you and Todd and everything, and it made me realize that I was out of line. About accusing you of hitting Todd."

Steve whistled in surprise. "I should have let you try on these goggles a lot earlier," he commented, holding them up for inspection. "They clearly have powers beyond limiting alcohol consumption in teenagers."

"Very funny," Victoria said. She swallowed. "Anyway, for what it's worth, I'm sorry."

"Damn," said Steve. He pulled her closer so that his face hovered above hers. "If I'd known apologizing would make you so attractive, I never would have invited Claire Timms to the ball with me."

Victoria felt like she had been slapped.

"Oh, you invited Claire?" She managed to sound nonchalant. "That's great."

He half-smiled. "You sure?"

"Of course," replied Victoria. She pulled away. She was conscious of a tugging ache beneath her rib cage. "What about Joe?"

Steve grabbed her arm to prevent her from walking away. "What do you mean, what about Joe?"

"I got the idea he was keen on Claire."

Steve smiled grimly. "Yeah, so did I," he said.

Victoria's eyes narrowed. "You're using Claire, aren't you?" she asked suddenly.

"Of course not."

"Yes, you are," she insisted. "You thought by asking her out, you could score off Joe at the same time. You've never liked him, ever since he used to follow Becky around, and you hated that Claire favored him the other day in the shops rather than you."

Steve scoffed. "That's ridiculous. I know the real reason why you're so angry." He held her gaze. "Admit it. You're not worried about Joe. You're jealous!"

Victoria laughed. "Now you're being ridiculous." She shook herself free from his hold and walked out, head up high, to the bathroom. When she was finally alone, she sat down on the toilet seat and burst into tears. Had she lost him forever?

CHAPTER 24

Victoria was too restless that evening to settle down.

"For heaven's sake, leave your phone alone," Janet said, staggering through into the living room with a huge pile of men's clothes. "He's not going to contact you more quickly if you keep staring at it."

"I never want to speak to him again," Victoria said. She tossed the phone aside.

Janet nodded. "Which explains why you keep checking your messages," she said. "Come and give me a hand here."

"Are you throwing Blake out?" Victoria gasped in awe at the pile of clothing.

"Of course not! But he's a hoarder, so while he and the kids are safely out of the house, I'm going to sort through all his things and donate his old stuff to the local clothing sale. What do you think of this? Too old, or do you think that this rip could be mended?"

Victoria blinked at the jeans. "Won't Blake be angry if he comes home to find half his clothes gone?"

"He won't even notice," said Janet. "There's stuff here from way back. I found a receipt from 2012 in one pocket."

"Okay, I take back what I said," Victoria told her. "The man clearly has a problem. Here, let me help you. Shall I put stuff to give away over here? I'll get a bag to put it in."

After half an hour, they had amassed a sizable bag of clothing, dating back, Janet insisted, to Blake's college days.

"If you're still full of nervous energy, how about taking this stuff down the road to the Meeting House for me?" asked Janet. "I'll get dinner ready in the meantime."

"Deal," replied Victoria. She hoisted up the bag and threw it over her shoulder.

By the time she had dropped off the clothes and left the building, the street was quiet, and Victoria glanced to the left and right nervously as she set off. *It's just Main Street,* she reminded herself, *not Chicago. You'll be fine.*

She halted as she heard voices from behind the Meeting House. Maybe it would be more sensible to walk part of the way with whoever was there if they were also heading home. She went around the building to see who was talking.

"Todd?" she muttered in surprise. The war vet was talking to someone that she couldn't see from her vantage point. Todd was unusually animated, his amiable face flushed and excitable. She saw he was holding a beer bottle in one hand, its contents half full.

"I saw you," Todd was saying to someone. He repeated himself, his voice rising. "I saw you on the trail, bending over her body, didn't I? That was you, wasn't it? And it was you who gave me that note for the detective. Wasn't it?"

Victoria, her pulse racing, crept a little closer. The other person said something in a low tone, and Todd gesticulated angrily. "Thought that would make you take notice," he said. "Yes, you are listening now, aren't you?"

An inaudible question from the other person made Todd pause, and then he took a draught from the bottle in his hand.

"I liked Rebecca," the beggar said sorrowfully. "She was always kind. Not like you. Not like you at all."

Victoria placed her hand over her mouth and crouched down behind a bush.

"I saw her scarf lying on the ground. I tried to put it over her to keep her warm while I went to get help, but—" The beggar paused and took another drink. "Then I realized she was dead."

Todd wiped his mouth with his hand and drank again. "I was scared. I was standing there alone with her, with my hands on her scarf, and I was scared. I knew no one would believe me when I told them what I had seen. They would just lock me up and say I did it. So I took the scarf instead. I forgot about the beer bottle. I wasn't thinking straight."

Then his face changed, and he set his mouth. "But now her sister is here. She won't give up. She will believe me."

The voice muttered something, and Todd stumbled forward as he bent toward the person to listen. "How much?" Todd asked, his usually vague voice sharp in his excitement. "No, I want more. Much more money. What is your life worth? What is it worth to you?"

Suddenly, Victoria saw the other person's arms reach out to grab Todd, and the air was split by a scream, a terrifying, rasping scream that chilled Victoria to the marrow.

"Stop!" yelled Victoria, leaping up.

She started running toward them, just as Todd's companion snatched the beer bottle from his hand, and smashed it over the beggar's head, leaving him in an inanimate heap.

Victoria tripped over a rock on the path and came down with a tumble. She pushed herself up, wincing, dimly aware that tomorrow she would be scratched and bruised. She raced over to where Todd was lying and caught a glimpse of a figure in the distance sprinting away.

She knelt over the body of the man. "Todd! Todd! Can you hear me?" she shouted. Shattered glass lay all around him, and a large, bleeding cut zigzagged its ugly route across his forehead. Another deep cut was oozing blood from the back of his head where he had fallen.

There was no response from the man, and she felt frantically for a pulse. She felt the faintest throb with her fingers and said a silent thank you. With trembling hands, she took out her phone and called Steve's cell. No reply. She tried Karen Timms. No answer. Where was everyone? She pulled off the long-sleeved sweater she had tied around her waist and held it to the cut on Todd's forehead. She was too scared to leave him in case his attacker returned, and she didn't want to stop compressing the cut.

"Help!" she shouted at the top of her voice while with her free hand she scrolled through her phone for Karen's number. "Anyone? Help!"

"V-Victoria?" she heard a familiar voice say, and she glanced up to see Joe, slightly stooped and an anxious frown above the heavy glasses, hastening toward her, followed by Claire Timms.

Claire gasped. "What happened?" she asked, hurrying forward. "We were just out walking."

"T-Todd has been badly injured," Victoria stammered. "Someone tried to kill him."

"I'll call my mom," Claire exclaimed, pulling out her phone.

"There's no answer from her or from Steve's cell," Victoria replied. Her stomach lurched as she put her fingers on Todd's pulse again and felt it weakening further.

At that moment, Karen phoned Claire back, and she spoke hurriedly to her.

"Mom's coming," Claire said. "She'll bring the car to the Meeting House."

Joe helped Victoria to rise and steered her away with a gentle touch on the arm. "Stand back," he said. "I'll carry him."

Joe was surprisingly strong and lifted Todd easily into his arms.

Claire took over holding Victoria's sweater to the beggar's forehead, and the three hurried out into Main Street as Karen pulled up in her SUV.

"What happened?" she exclaimed, leaping out. "Put him in my car. Why didn't you call for an ambulance?"

"I don't know, it all happened so fast. We couldn't get hold of you," Claire said as her mother flung open the doors for Joe.

"I left my phone at home," said Karen. She frowned as she leaned over the motionless form slumped in the seat.

"Is he still alive?" asked Claire, her voice trembling. Joe put his arm around her, and she held on to him gratefully.

Karen nodded. "Just." She glanced up at the three anxious faces staring at her. "If we get him to the hospital now, he may have a chance. Let's go!"

CHAPTER 25

The mood at the police station was tense.

"How is Todd?" asked Steve.

"Breathing," Victoria replied. "Barely. And no change in his condition."

"Did forensics reveal anything about his assailant?" asked Karen. She nodded at the report in Victoria's hand.

"This is the report for the attack on me at Norway Pond," she said, continuing to read. "Todd's report I've already read."

"Anything interesting in either?"

"Blood spatter analysis confirmed what I saw of the attack — a direct blow to Todd's head with a bottle. And of course he was badly hurt by the injury to the back of his head when he fell. I also have the results of a DNA sample from the attack on Todd and a sample of DNA from under my fingernails as well for my assailant."

"The same person I presume?"

Victoria glanced up. "That's the surprising thing. The results from the two tests show that the attacks were carried out by two different people."

"Two people involved?" puzzled Karen. "Were both assailants involved in Rebecca's murder then, and why?"

Victoria sat down, poring over the results. "That doesn't really make sense," she said. "The motives for Rebecca's murder seem to be either romantic jealousy or an argument. Doesn't make sense that either would be carried out by two people working together. I keep thinking and thinking who might have had the biggest motive."

Victoria closed her eyes trying to sort through the list of those who might conceivably have had something to do with Becky's murder. The names in her head went around and around in circles. She opened her eyes and found Steve watching her closely. She looked back, trying to read his mind. And at the center of it all was Becky. Young, beautiful, vibrant Becky, who smiled on everyone with the same kindness. *Then all smiles stopped together* . . . and the only one who knew who had done it was Todd. She had to keep him alive.

* * *

The walls of the police station felt like they were closing in on Victoria, and her head was pounding. Her tea sat cold and untouched on her desk. She stood up, stretching stiffly, and checked her phone. Two hours past the lunch break she hadn't taken. She had to get out. She grabbed her car keys and headed for the door.

* * *

Sarah's Hat Boxes.

Victoria stood gazing up at the shop sign with its black background, framed with a red margin and displaying in the middle a picture of three hat boxes, stacked in the fashion of a tiered cake.

She walked inside, feeling the heaviness lift as she revolved slowly on her heels to take in the multitude of hat boxes. Becky had loved it here. There were as many boxes as she remembered from her childhood. Round boxes, oval boxes, square boxes, boxes decorated with flowers, boxes with seashells, boxes with polka dots, boxes of every shade, from the blues of azure, laguna, navy and aqua to amethyst, burgundy, cerise and flamingo pink.

She tried to imagine what she would have bought for Becky and stared at the shelf in front of her, torn between an oval box with blue starfish and a white box with a black rim displaying the Eiffel Tower.

"I would choose the starfish," a voice said in her ear, and she jumped.

"Steve! What are you doing here?"

He shrugged.

"I saw your car as I drove past and came in out of curiosity. Are you going to a wedding?" He lifted a cylindrical ribboned wedding box of white moire and held it up for her inspection.

"Put it down," Victoria hissed. "You'll get fingerprints on it."

He grinned and returned it to the shelf.

"You haven't answered my question yet," he said.

"I came here as a child," she replied. "I just wanted to see it again. Maybe buy a box as a memento." *To feel close to Becky again.*

He took her by the elbow and leaned across her to point at a box in the corner.

"What about that one?"

His closeness made her dizzy. Victoria realized she was holding her breath and forced herself to exhale.

"Something wrong?" she heard Steve's voice say teasingly.

His eyes glistened with a playfulness that made her feel breathless again.

"I like that one," she managed. It was a tiny box, striped in the colors of the rainbow.

She reached out for it, but Steve lifted it off the shelf himself.

"Allow me," he said with a wink.

"What? No, you can't — I don't need — you really don't have to."

"I know," Steve steered her to the counter and took out his wallet. He turned to her once he had paid and placed the box in her hands.

"A peace offering for calling you jealous," he said.

"Thank you," she replied, moved, raising her eyes to his. She thought of Becky again and how much she had loved her rainbow-colored scarf. She hoped her voice sounded steady. "It's beautiful. This is exactly what I would have chosen." *For you, Becky.*

"If it's beautiful, then it suits you," he replied.

* * *

Even Victoria finally succumbed to the thrill of the ball when Janet wouldn't take no for an answer.

"What do you think?" she demanded, spinning in front of Janet on her stilettos. Victoria's sleek satin dress, ebony and ankle-length, with a daring slit up one side, clung to each curve in true secret-agent fashion.

"Beautiful," grunted Janet, who was trying to do up a zip on a dress she'd last worn before having children. "Help me here. I may need surgery to get out of this again."

"Breathe in," Victoria laughed. She zipped her friend in at last, stood back and gave her a thumbs up. "Blake is going to be sorry he's only arriving tomorrow."

When they arrived at the country club where the ball was being held, it was already flooded with people, the murmur of conversation intermingling with music from a live band playing light classics.

"Isn't that 'Moon River' they're playing?" said Victoria.

"Could be. I love violins," commented Janet. She caught the eye of one of the musicians and smiled as she passed. "What a mass of people. There must be over a hundred here already."

The ballroom, used often as a wedding venue, fitted the crowds comfortably. Guests sat chatting around circular tables decorated with glass vases holding multicolored roses or stood in excited huddles beneath the high ceiling, from which golden chandeliers hung. Waiters weaved their way across the floor, offering snacks and strawberry rosé punch.

"Shrimp cocktail, Swedish meatballs, oysters, crab cakes . . . I'm in heaven," declared Janet, her fingers hovering indecisively over the hors d'oeuvres.

Under the chandeliers, the men looked suave in Bond-like suits, and the ladies shimmered in the light, some in skintight miniskirts, others in chiffon that swayed with each movement, revealing toy revolvers strapped to their thighs.

"Itchy feet?" asked Janet as she saw Victoria nodding to the music.

"Shall we dance?" asked an oily voice, and Victoria turned to see Maurice, flashy in an expensive suit, holding out his hand.

Out of the corner of her eye, she saw Steve pulling Claire onto the dance floor. Victoria suppressed a pang as she realized for the first time how beautiful Claire was. Petite and timid and so ready to admire someone as confident and charming as Steve.

"Why not?" she replied, taking Maurice's hand.

Maurice held her close, his breath hot against her neck, and she fought the panic that rose up within her. She felt her chest tighten. She couldn't breathe, and her head felt sickeningly dizzy.

"Spin me," she ordered. Anything to get away from the clammy clasp of the man.

He spun her out, and as she spiraled, she noticed Steve watching her, a jealous gleam in his eye.

"You look gorgeous," Maurice wheezed, a little out of breath from the exercise as he drew her closer.

"All for a good cause," she said. "Spin me again!"

He chuckled. "You're a little exhibitionist, aren't you?" She gave an involuntary shudder and almost bumped into Steve.

"The next dance is mine," Steve murmured in her ear, leaving her fuming that he hadn't even bothered to ask her.

The music ended, and Victoria gratefully withdrew her hand from Maurice's. Steve, she noted, was still preoccupied with saying something to Claire, laughing as he teased her. Not that she cared at all. She felt a light tap on her shoulder.

"I'd have known you for a spy anywhere," John remarked, smiling down at her. She colored, annoyed with herself for noticing how well his black jacket and white-button shirt suited his broad-shouldered form. He proffered his hand questioningly as the next song began. She hesitated, then, as she saw Steve striding confidently toward her, nodded at John and placed her hand in his. He held her hand lightly, leaving enough space between them that she felt able to relax. Following her gaze, he smiled ruefully.

"Are you using me to make him jealous?" John asked, lifting her effortlessly off her feet as they turned a corner. She felt lighter than air, as though she were flying.

"I suppose so," she admitted, "but I would have danced with you anyway."

His foot slid slightly, and he involuntarily held her to his chest to regain his balance. She could feel his muscles, hard and comfortingly powerful, through his shirt.

"Sorry, too close," he muttered, hastily releasing her. She was both relieved and, at the same time, oddly disappointed.

He looked up over her head to where Steve was glowering at them. "Your technique is working," he commented. "He's ready to wring my neck."

John nodded at Maurice, now standing next to his wife. "Did you notice?"

She looked at him questioningly.

"Look at his sleeve as we dance past," was all John would say, steering her in that direction. He slowed as they neared Maurice, and as they danced past him, he lifted his hand to his mouth to cough. Victoria blinked, startled.

"The cufflink. It's identical to the one we found."

"Maybe he has several pairs," John replied. "You think he was down there at Norway Pond?"

"And was connected to the assault?" Victoria completed his thought. "I suppose it could easily be someone else's, or he could have lost it another time, but he's slimeball enough for anything."

"I'd watch my back if I were you," John recommended as the music faded and Steve approached them.

"She's mine now, Gardner," he said coolly, taking her arm. "Let's get some air." She pulled away her arm but walked with him, a thrill tingling her spine. "We can talk better here," he said, leaning back against the trunk of a yellow birch outside the venue. A wooden table that had held drinks for arriving guests lay beneath it.

"You want to talk?" Victoria queried, her mind still half on Maurice's cufflink.

"Why, what did you have in mind?" he teased her, and she was grateful the evening dark hid her face. Then he was serious again, and his eyes appeared to her almost tender.

"I'm worried about you, Victoria. The attack on the homeless war vet, the attack on you — I don't know if you're safe here."

"What do you mean?" she said.

"Next time you might not be so lucky. You could be killed."

Victoria stared at him disbelievingly. "You aren't suggesting I quit, are you?"

"I would still work on the case," Steve said. "Give you regular updates. Come up to Chicago maybe."

The innuendo in these words brought the color back into her face, but she shook her head. "I need to be here."

Steve frowned.

"You don't trust me to solve it. Is that it?" he asked. "You honestly think you need to be here?"

Victoria was needled by the accusatory tone. "She's my sister, Steve! So yes, I think I need to be here! I refuse to leave until I have justice for her. Why would you ask me if I am going?"

Steve leaped forward and dashed aside the table between them, his eyes blazing.

"You want to know the real reason I asked?" he demanded, his volume raising, and Victoria straightened too, equally angry and slightly frightened.

"Yes, Steve, yes," she said. "Yes, I want to know."

The next moment, his arms were around her and her back was pressed up against the tree trunk. Bending his head, he kissed her, not the tentative brief kiss of the other night, but one so intimate and passionate that her head reeled. Her first instinct was to push him away, but it had been so many years since she had allowed anyone near her, and the touch of his lips on hers drove all sense of sanity from her. Instead, she found herself entwining her arms around his neck and pulling him closer, her heart thudding wildly. He finally released her, his chest rising and falling rapidly.

"That is why," he said huskily, his hands cradling her face.

"I'm not leaving," she whispered. She drew him to her again. "We're in this together, Steve."

CHAPTER 26

"Home at last!" called a voice to Janet from the doorway of her home, and a stocky, dark-haired man staggered in, laden with suitcases, followed by a wildly unkempt puppy. Victoria watched as two young children shoved past their father and flung themselves at Janet.

"What is that?" Janet demanded, hoisting her four-year-old son onto her knee and pointing to the doorway.

"My dog!" Harvey said proudly.

"*Our* dog," corrected seven-year-old Carrie, pulling a face at her brother. "She's ours!"

"Say hello to my friend Vicky," said Janet, and both children grinned up at Victoria.

"Hello," they chorused, and Harvey gave a shy wave.

"I mentioned the puppy to you, didn't I?" Blake said sheepishly. He kissed his wife.

Janet stared at the overgrown pile of fur panting its way toward them. The dog's shaggy coat was a glorious mixture of mocha and caramel shades, and her parentage was clearly indeterminate. Her long collie-like tail fanned out as she thumped it on the ground, her ears drooped in the manner of a beagle, and her legs were those of an Afghan hound, her paws almost invisible below mountains of fur. She crouched on the carpet and made a large puddle, then flopped down by their feet.

"That is *not* a puppy," Janet responded emphatically. "It is a floor mop with a tongue and no bladder control, and we're taking her to the vet before she produces a string of little floor mops that eat us out of house and home."

Harvey pulled a face at his sister and mouthed, "She's *my* dog!"

"Mommy, Harvey's not sharing and caring! He's a pig!" shouted Carrie, pulling a face back.

"You were telling me about the joys of settling down the other day?" Victoria murmured to Janet.

"They were away camping at the time," Janet defended herself. "I was delusional. Reality all came flooding back the moment they returned with a hair-shedding mutt in tow." She looked severely at Blake who muttered something and refused to meet her eye. "You know we need to register her at the town clerk's office?"

"I'll go to the clerk and give you time to unpack," offered Victoria. "They're open till eight, right?"

"Yes, thank you," Janet said gratefully. "You're a lifesaver. I'm going to phone John Gardner in the meantime and make an appointment to have her sterilized. Just pick up the forms or the gold tag or whatever it is that we need to register and license this hound. Otherwise, we have to pay for each month we're late."

"No problem."

Victoria waved as she drove away, hiding a smile at the ensuing chaos that seemed to be typical of Janet's family. A few minutes later, she had parked and was strolling across the large expanse of grass toward the office. *If only Chicago felt this spacious*, she couldn't help thinking, remembering her apartment in Morgan Park nostalgically. Her phone rang.

"Steve. Hi." She hoped she didn't sound as breathless as she felt.

"So, how's my favorite girlfriend?"

Girlfriend. The word still sounded foreign, *felt* foreign, to her and evoked connotations that were slightly intoxicating and dangerous.

"Want to meet up this evening?" he asked.

"At the hospital? I'm going there soon if I have enough time."

"I want to be alone with you."

Remembering the thrill of his touch, she smiled but simultaneously was aware of a choking anxiety.

"Not tonight, Steve. I'm sorry." She paused. "I'll miss you."

"I'll miss you too." The words came so casually, so smoothly, off his tongue, as though they were traveling a well-worn path. How many times had he said them before?

Inside the clerk's office, there were only a few others waiting to be helped. The woman at the front of the line turned around and gave a nervous start. Megan Jenkins. What was wrong with the woman? Several times, she half-turned as though she wanted to speak to Victoria. Once Victoria had finished at the clerk's office, she hurried out across the grass back to her car, hoping she would have time to go to the hospital to see Todd before dinner. She checked her phone. There wasn't really time, but she had to see him. She quickly messaged Janet to tell her why she would be late and pulled out her car keys.

"Detective," a voice called out, and Victoria halted, her driver's door already open. "Can I talk to you?"

Megan. She must have been waiting for her.

The woman was twisting her handbag between restless fingers. "Your throat," she said hoarsely. "Is it okay? Can we talk?"

"I can't chat now," Victoria said, impatient to be gone. "Can it wait?"

Megan touched Victoria's neck fleetingly, her eyes widening. Victoria flinched at the contact.

"I must tell you," Megan said. She swallowed, then drew back as her husband pulled up in an expensive Mercedes to pick her up. "Later," she added under her breath.

"About what?" demanded Victoria, suddenly intrigued.

"About my husband's business interests," she whispered, "and the money he stole."

CHAPTER 27

"Has there been any change, Sister Lemmer?" Victoria asked the nurse on duty.

"Not much," replied the sister, a squat, sour-faced individual who despised all doctors on principle. She glanced in Victoria's direction with apparent lack of interest, barely lifting her eyes to her face. Victoria's eyes twinkled. Old Mother Hen, she had been told, was what the other nurses called Greta Lemmer, or sometimes, in less complimentary tones, Sister Lemon — acerbic to her core with no time to waste on niceties. She had, as everyone in the hospital knew, probably saved more lives than most of the doctors on the floor.

"He woke briefly yesterday," Sister Lemmer conceded, tearing her attention away from her patient, whose blood pressure she was checking, to address the interloper. "And muttered a little."

"He spoke?" demanded a voice from behind them, and Victoria turned to the familiar figure whose large frame towered over them.

"Steve!" she exclaimed. "You came!" She touched Sister Lemmer lightly on her sleeve. "What words? What did he say?" she asked.

Sister Lemmer, who had turned back to Todd, glanced around in annoyance. "Not much that made sense," she replied. "Once he muttered 'scarf' and then 'Eve'."

"Eve?" Victoria was mystified. "Why Eve? Even? Adam and Eve?"

Sister Lemmer didn't think this was worth a reply. She ignored her and noted the blood-pressure reading from the screen attached to Todd's bed.

At that moment, a faint groan came from the bed. Todd opened his eyes to find three faces peering over his bed rail at him.

"Todd, it's Victoria," the young detective said, nervously tapping the bed rail with her fingers.

Todd looked up at her vaguely and then across to the others. For a moment, no emotion registered, and then suddenly, recognition dawned. His hands started tearing at the bedclothes in agitation, as though he wanted to get up, but he was too weak and uncoordinated still to do more than flail around in the bed. Realizing it, he sank down onto his pillows, and his fingers crept up the bed rail till they lay over those of Victoria. She forced herself not to withdraw her hand and sat down on the closest chair so that he could see her more easily.

"Todd, we need you to tell us about the murder of my sister," she said urgently, maintaining eye contact. "And the person you went to see behind the Meeting House. We want to know what happened."

Todd nodded and coughed so hard his eyes watered. "Eve," he muttered hoarsely. "Eve."

"It was evening," Victoria said to the others, glancing at them. "I think 'eve' means evening."

Todd became more agitated, his fingernails digging into Victoria's hand so hard she thought he was going to draw blood.

"Blood pressure spiking," Sister Lemmer said severely, glaring at Victoria.

"We won't be a minute," she said. "Todd, can you remember who it was that you met that evening who tried to kill you?"

Todd was about to speak when another coughing fit attacked him. He lifted himself up on one elbow in an effort to support himself.

"Money," he whispered, his face pasty from exhaustion. "The money."

His eyelids sank and he fell back. Sister Lemmer clicked her tongue.

"He's gone again," she muttered. "Not good." She bustled around him, drawing the curtains and gesturing them out with an impatient flick of the hand.

"What on earth did that mean?" Victoria said to Steve.

"Simple. He wanted money from someone that evening," Steve replied tensely, his eyes on the dividing curtain. "For keeping quiet about what he knew."

Sister Lemmer emerged a few minutes later, her face characteristically grim.

"When do you think he will wake up again?" asked Victoria.

The nurse shook her head.

"Maybe tomorrow, maybe the day after." She paused for a moment. "Maybe never."

* * *

"Where are you parked?" Steve asked, as they left the hospital.

"Just over there." Victoria gestured with her hand. "So, I'll see you at work tomorrow then?"

She could just make out his smile in the darkness before she felt him put his arm through hers.

"May I walk you to your vehicle, ma'am?"

"You don't have to." She didn't sound very convincing.

"But I want to."

Warmth spread across her chest and her hand traveled, unconsciously, to her neck.

"You do?"

He laughed.

"Come, Detective Wharton. The longer you take, the longer I have to wait before kissing you goodbye."

Victoria wasn't sure whether she was more grateful for the darkness for hiding her blushing cheeks or the breeze for cooling her face.

"I was so pleased when you arrived tonight," she said. Admitting even a vulnerability so trivial, she felt stripped to the core.

"Hey, I can feel you trembling. Is it that cold?" He removed his arm from hers to pull her closer. "Better?"

"Much."

"I'm glad I came tonight too."

There was a note in Steve's voice she hadn't heard before, and she placed her head on his shoulder briefly. *Had he come specially to see her?*

"Do you think Todd is going to make it?" she asked.

"Who knows? I have my doubts. What do you think?"

"He must," Victoria said fiercely. "He is the one person who could give us answers."

"Too bad he didn't tell us what he knew when he had the chance," Steve replied.

"It's been driving me crazy," she agreed. "To think that the person who could tell us what happened when Becky died was right there in front of us, and yet we still don't know anything."

She paused.

"Not only that but — if he dies, the case dies with him. We have to keep him alive, Steve. We've *got to.*"

She shivered again suddenly.

"Hey," said Steve caressingly and took her hands. "Take a deep breath."

She inhaled, then laughed jerkily.

"I'm okay. I think. Hey, here's my car," she said, trying to control her shaking voice.

"So, I guess it's been a pretty tough night for you. Will you be all right to drive home on your own, or would you like me to take you? I can always ask Karen to bring me by the hospital tomorrow to fetch my car?"

"You'd do that for me?"

"Sure."

Victoria swallowed back tears.

"Thanks, Steve. That means such a lot to me." *You have no idea how much.* She took another breath and stepped away, half turning her back to him to open her car door. "I'll be fine though."

"I'll say goodnight then." She felt his jacket brush against her sleeve as he moved closer. She felt heat flaming into her chest again as his arms encircled her and she felt him kissing her neck. Her muscles tensed first at the contact then relaxed. She turned in his embrace to face him, placing her arms around his neck.

"You know, I wasn't too sure at first what I was doing when we decided to give this relationship a chance," she admitted.

"Yeah, I got the feeling you were a bit nervous."

Victoria laughed, embarrassed. "There hasn't been anyone for a long time."

"No? Those Chicago guys really missed their chance."

"No, no. I mean, it was my choice. You know, I was focusing on work." *And terrified to let anyone close, terrified of the nightmarish memories of my father that seemed to surface whenever I risked a relationship.*

"And now? How do you feel about us?"

In reply, she reached up and kissed him.

"Does that answer your question?" she asked breathlessly.

He laughed and pulled her closer.

"Maybe you should tell me one more time, just to be sure I understood you. What do you think?"

She nodded wordlessly, hoping he could see her in the night shadows, and he bent his head to hers, kissing her cheek, her lips, her neck.

"I'm glad I waited so long to find someone like you," she murmured.

She stepped back slightly and glanced up at him shyly. "And you?"

"I'm also glad you waited to find someone like me," he joked.

"No, I mean—" she wasn't sure how to word it. "I don't want to intrude. I mean, I guess there have been a lot of girls before me."

"Not that many," Steve replied, taking her hand.

"Has it also been a long time for you?"

"Much too long," he answered quickly.

"I just thought—"

"You think too much, Detective Wharton," he said, his finger touching her cheek as he kissed her. "You know that?"

"Right now, I can hardly think at all," she murmured.

"Hey, you know what? Same here," he said. "And right now, I'd rather not be thinking. What do you say?"

"Good idea, Detective McCade," she whispered, kissing him again.

* * *

Victoria parked outside the vet's surgery and got out of the car slowly, regretting her offer to fetch Harvey and Carrie's overly boisterous puppy — whom they had named Belle — after her sterilization. Janet had argued that 'The Beast' was a more appropriate name if they were going with fairy tales but had been outvoted.

The waiting room was almost empty.

"Claire, is Janet Mitchley's dog ready for collection?" asked Victoria.

Claire Timms smiled awkwardly and looked away. "I'll check," she murmured, hurrying away to avoid chatting. What was wrong with the girl? Before Victoria had time to analyze the matter, Claire had returned. "Come through, please. She's here."

Victoria followed her to where Belle was being kept. The enormous puppy flung herself onto Victoria, so thrilled that it seemed not only her tail but her entire mop-like body was wagging itself. She didn't seem to be subdued by her operation one bit.

"Who needs a husband if you've got a welcome like this waiting for you at home?" laughed Victoria, trying not to overbalance as Belle threw herself at her rescuer. "No licking my face, please!"

Claire looked wistfully at Victoria. "A husband would still be nice," she said, a slight catch in her voice, and Victoria frowned. Why was Claire so down? *Steve.* The answer leaped out at her suddenly. She'd been so caught up in the craziness of the past few weeks that she'd forgotten how Claire worshipped him. But how did she know? Had Karen worked it out and told her?

"You're much too young to get married," a voice interrupted her thoughts. "Your boss forbids it for at least another six months. It's in your contract."

Claire looked around to see John standing in the doorway, pulling off surgical gloves. He grinned at her, and she managed a faint smile and squeezed past him, hurrying back to her desk.

John's grin faded as he stepped into the room. "When was your boyfriend going to bother to tell her that you are together?" he demanded. "I mean, just the other day, it was her he was trying to impress. She was so excited to go to that ball with him — she could talk about nothing else."

Victoria shook her head. "It all just happened very suddenly, I guess."

John stared out of the window, his hands on his hips. "Very suddenly," he replied under his breath. "Claire had been meaning to ask him to the Shakespeare show that's happening at the Hancock Inn. Instead, she ended up crying at her desk." He paused. "I didn't even know you were together until she told me."

"Why should you?" demanded Victoria, annoyed. "What's it to you anyway, who I date? It's none of your business."

"Maybe you and your boyfriend suit each other pretty well after all," John answered. "You don't care who you hurt, do you?"

"How did I hurt you?" Victoria said, the volume of her voice rising.

"I'm not talking about myself. I'm talking about Claire. You couldn't have made her feel more of an idiot if you'd tried. Claire told me you got together on the evening of the ball at which Steve was supposed to be partnering her."

"He was! He did!" protested Victoria. "It wasn't like they were a couple."

John didn't bother to reply to her.

"Can I take Belle?" Victoria snapped, her voice catching. Her eyes blurred with tears.

He gestured to her to take the dog, and she scooped her carefully up into her arms, grateful for her softness.

She brushed past him at the door.

"I thought I knew you."

The words were spoken so quietly that Victoria wouldn't have heard if she hadn't been listening for them, for anything, from him.

She turned to look at John. "Yeah? Well, I thought I knew you too." She bit her lip, staring at him across the hurt dividing them. "I thought you were my friend."

John stared back at her, with no sign of the warm smile or the dimple that appeared when he was teasing her. "What friend would I be if I kept quiet, Vicky?" he muttered. "To you or to Claire?"

He sank down onto one of the empty dog cages, his shoulders hunched over so the unruly copper of his hair covered his face. "I wouldn't have bothered to say anything to you," he said simply, "if I didn't care."

The silence between them stretched till Victoria could bear it no longer.

"Goodbye, John," she replied. The sound of her voice echoed in her ears. It sounded very final.

* * *

Once at the police station, Victoria pulled up Megan Jenkins's number on her cell phone.

"Answer your phone, Megan," she muttered. "Come on. You know you want to talk to me."

"Why would she want to speak with you?" asked Officer Karen Timms curiously, overhearing Victoria.

"Some dirt in Maurice's past."

It was at this inopportune moment that Megan's husband walked in, accompanied by Steve.

"Maurice!" exclaimed Victoria.

Seeing the two together accentuated to Victoria everything that Maurice was not. Steve's supple leanness and the hardness of his toned body made her swallow with pride. *He's mine*, she thought.

Maurice shoved his hands into his pockets, and strode back and forth as though trying to gain his composure.

"Where is the boy?" he snapped at last.

"Your son, Gavin?" Karen asked, perplexed. "How would we know?"

Maurice stopped in his tracks at the genuine confusion in her voice. "You really don't know, do you?" he said. "The boy has been gone since last night."

"Why would you assume we knew where he was?" asked Karen.

Maurice tried to collect himself and managed a glimmer of the old charm. "I've spoken to you privately about the boy before," he said, addressing Victoria. "I think the time has come for complete frankness."

"That would be nice," Victoria muttered.

"Gavin, as you know, is a compulsive liar. Last night, we had an altercation, and I said—" Maurice smiled ruefully at them, a somewhat calculated smile, intended, Victoria was sure, to win them over. "We all say what we regret in the heat of the moment," he continued. "Gavin threatened me. Said he was going to discredit me and go to the police. Then he stormed out."

"And you thought we had taken him in?"

Maurice shrugged. "He can be very persuasive."

“We’ll do what we can to trace your son, Mr. Jenkins,” said Steve.

“Thank you,” Maurice replied. “My wife and I hoped he’d spent the night at a friend’s and weren’t overly worried. Till now.”

CHAPTER 28

"Hurry *up*, Vicky!" shouted Carrie, tugging her along while trying to stop Belle pulling in the opposite direction. "Pick Belle up, Harvey."

"Where are we going?" protested Victoria.

"Just around the common," Harvey said, tucking Belle under his arm, where she wriggled like a toddler throwing a tantrum. "Mom says that Belle needs lots of exercise."

"I agree," Victoria said, examining her gnawed sneakers. Belle had discovered them under the bed that morning after a night of remorseless destruction that had left the living-room curtains ripped partially off their railing.

Victoria jogged along with the children as far as the common, and then flopped down onto the grass. "Why don't you walk Belle in the direction of the war memorial over there?" she suggested, hoping to get a few minutes' breather.

"Hey, there's the vet with his dog!" shouted Carrie, waving enthusiastically. Victoria wished she could vanish into the ground. "And his friend with the Adam's apple."

Victoria noted, with amusement, as John and Joe neared them, that the latter did have a protruding Adam's apple.

Joe slowed down and smiled his usual nervous grin as they came abreast, but John merely nodded at Victoria in greeting, though he gave the children a wink.

"She's looking in good shape, kids," John said, his dimple showing slightly as Carrie demonstrated how she was teaching Belle to sit.

"Vicky?" asked Harvey, puzzled.

"Your dog," John said flatly. He barely glanced at Victoria. "I'm going to give St. Patrick a quick run. Back in a minute, Joe."

"C-congratulations," Joe stammered to Victoria.

"For what?" Victoria said bitterly, turning her back on John as he jogged off.

"I h-hear you and Steve are an item."

Heat rose in her cheeks as she flushed. "Did Claire tell you?"

Joe grimaced. "John told me. I h-haven't seen much of Claire recently."

Victoria sighed. "You should, Joe. Maybe ask her to the Shakespeare play that's coming up soon?"

He shook his head vigorously. "I'm no c-competition for someone like Steve," he said. "W-who was I kidding?"

"But seeing Steve is with me now, you have a chance with Claire," said Vicky. She smiled what she hoped was an encouraging smile, and her fingers intertwined and released as she waited for his response. She had to make this right, somehow.

Joe's head jerked involuntarily, and he blinked rapidly in embarrassment. "Not as h-her second choice," he murmured, "even I deserve better."

The usual self-deprecatory smile was so vulnerable that Victoria felt moved to say, "*Particularly* you, Joe."

They say for a few minutes in an awkward silence. Victoria was relieved when Carrie came running over.

"Hey, Joe, look what Belle can do," shouted Carrie, and Joe knelt beside the puppy to watch her do a trick that consisted mostly of Carrie shouting commands that Belle blithely ignored while she tried to pull the laces out of the little girl's shoes.

"She'll get there in the end," said a slightly breathless voice in her ear, and Victoria turned to see John drop down onto the grass beside her. St. Patrick hurried over to join the children and Belle. "She's still a puppy."

Victoria stared down at her damaged sneakers. "That's what worries me," she muttered. "I think I need to take her to yoga to calm down. Either yoga or exorcism. Both could work."

John grinned, and for a moment the tension between them dissipated. "My mom goes to yoga on the shore of Norway Pond," he said. "You should try it."

"Maybe I will," Victoria replied. She smiled awkwardly.

John smiled back in silence, the tension returning.

"Come on guys, we'd better get going," Victoria said, getting up and dusting off her jeans. An impulse grabbed her. She turned to Joe.

"Ducks," she said suddenly.

"Ducks?"

Victoria nodded. "Ring-necked ducks. In the pond in Janet's back garden. I know you've been doing research on them."

Joe's hands were a flurry of excitement as he dug in every available pocket for his phone. "Are you sure? It is n-not even fall yet," he stammered. He finally unearthed his phone and showed her a picture.

"Is that what you saw?"

John, watching her closely, saw Victoria's hand tremble slightly before she shoved it into her pocket.

"Looks familiar," said Victoria, assuaging her conscience by assuring herself that all ducks did, in fact, look alike. "Want to come look tomorrow after work? About six?"

"Th-thank you." Joe glanced at John. "You going to join me investigating the ring-necks, John? It's highly unusual, what she's describing."

John glanced at Victoria, frowning. "You go first and report back," he suggested.

Joe glanced from John to Victoria but said nothing other than, "Will do. Thanks, Victoria. Are we on our way, John?"

"With you in a minute, Joe," the young vet replied. "Why don't you help the kids walk Belle to the bandstand and back?"

Joe's eyes, sharp behind the thick glasses, registered the silent request, and he nodded.

"C-come on, guys," he said, "I'll race you."

Victoria tried to breathe slowly. *No more arguing*, she pleaded silently. She'd had enough.

"What's your game, Victoria?" John asked.

She sighed. "No games," she replied. "At least, nothing underhand. I just want to make amends to those I've hurt. Joe. Claire."

Comprehension showed in his face. "How about if I send Claire around with the invoice for Belle's op?" he asked, and she saw the faintest glimmer of a twinkle in his eyes. "Our internet connection has been intermittent, so probably best not to try emailing it."

"Would you?" asked Victoria. "I know I'm probably interfering, but I can't bear how unhappy I've made her. Unintentionally."

John shrugged. "Maybe occasional interference is justifiable." He smiled, and she breathed a sigh of relief.

"I'm really sorry, John," she said, her shoulders jerking slightly.

"Hey, you're not crying, are you?" he exclaimed, pulling her to him as he put an arm around her. He stopped as he felt her stiffen.

"Sorry, I wasn't thinking," he said. "May I give you a hug?"

She nodded, the automatic anxiety she always felt dissipating as he held her gently. As a friend would. Almost.

A sharp intake of breath made Victoria look up, and she broke away hurriedly. "Steve!" she exclaimed, embarrassed.

"Victoria," he replied, though he kept his eyes fixed on John. "Want to tell me what the hell is going on?"

John released Victoria and shrugged, turning away.

"Don't turn your back on me," Steve snapped, glaring at the back of his head.

John turned back to meet his gaze. "Or what?"

"Steve, please, it was really nothing but a friendly hug," Victoria said, rubbing her neck tiredly and stretching it from side to side.

"Yoga." John smiled at her, gesturing at her stiff neck. "Norway Pond. Don't forget."

Steve started forward as Victoria's phone suddenly rang.

"Thank you," she whispered under her breath, seeing Steve pause and his clenched fingers relax slightly at the interruption. "Hi, who is this?"

She straightened up suddenly, her tiredness gone, and grabbed Steve's hand.

"To the hospital, quick!" she exclaimed. "Todd has been attacked!"

CHAPTER 29

Victoria and Steve were shown into a small office by the doctor on duty, Dr Anderson, and Sister Lemmer was summoned.

"Last night there was a fire alarm when a storeroom caught alight," Dr Anderson began. "In hindsight, the fire was presumably the work of the perpetrator. In the confusion, a person attacked Todd as he was being wheeled out to the emergency exit." She gestured toward Sister Lemmer. "It's thanks to Sister here that Todd is, currently, still alive."

Sister Lemmer didn't appear at all moved by this tribute. She herself was in the wars, with a large bandage on one arm and a dressing on her cheek. She sat squarely in her chair, her hands in her lap, and glared at each of the others in turn.

"Did you get a glimpse of the attacker?" Victoria asked her. "What happened when he — she — attacked?"

Sister Lemmer clenched her jaw.

"The person who tried to kill *my* patient," she said, with a clear emphasis on the possessive adjective, "was wearing a mask and armed with a kitchen knife of sorts. They attempted to push me out of the way and tried to slit my patient's throat."

"What did you do?" Steve asked.

Sister Lemmer shifted her arms slightly, and Victoria, catching a glimpse of her biceps, was grateful that Todd had such a powerful carer.

"I grappled with them," she said succinctly. "I mean *him*, almost certainly. They have very little courage, I find, when confronted," she added as though this sort of situation was a daily occurrence. Victoria banished a vision of Sister Lemmer gearing up for regular night-time battles, fighting off armed intruders each evening. The sister pointed to her bandaged cheek. "The coward tried to frighten me by slicing open my face and arm."

"You weren't frightened?" Victoria interposed. "What did you do?"

"I subdued him," Sister Lemmer replied, as though surprised Victoria should ask. "When he bent over my patient, I took him by the throat and rammed his head against the wall. After that, he appeared a little dizzy."

Victoria stared at Sister Lemmer in awe.

"She's a legend." Dr Anderson smiled briefly, checking Todd's file. "The infiltrator did manage to do a fair amount of damage to Todd, however, before escaping through the emergency exit. We have bandaged Todd up and are trying to keep him as quiet as possible, but there has been significant damage to his vocal cords, so he won't be able to speak for some time, and he has lost a great deal of blood."

"Is he conscious?" Steve asked.

Sister Lemmer shook her head.

"He won't be able to respond to anything at present," said Dr Anderson. "Your chief of police was here this morning to arrange with the hospital authorities for additional security for Todd until, we hope, he recovers and is able to communicate with us."

"Any evidence as to the perpetrator?"

"Big," said Sister Lemmer. "Very powerful."

"But not powerful enough to contend with you," Victoria said. Her eyes unexpectedly filled with tears. "You're an angel, Sister Lemmer."

Sister Lemmer glared ferociously back at Victoria, but her eyes glistened very slightly, and there was the tiniest hint of a smile.

"Just doing my job," she said. "If you need me, I'll be with my patient, making sure he doesn't get himself killed. *Men*," she added in disgust.

CHAPTER 30

The aching in Victoria's neck and temples drove her to take John's advice to try yoga on the sandy beach of Norway Pond before heading off to the police station for work. Yoga, she reflected, as she straightened out the beach towel that she'd been assured would serve for an exercise mat, might just be the thing to help calm her down right now.

"And downward-facing dog," she heard the tranquil tones of the instructor say, and she pushed herself up into the position, legs and arms straight, calves protesting as she attempted to keep her soles flat on the towel.

"Head down. Looking great, Victoria." Victoria tried to grin in response but only managed a grimace as her calves accustomed themselves to the unfamiliar exercise.

Paula Gardner, John's mother, was stretching beside her, and she smiled at Victoria too and gave her a thumbs up. Victoria managed to reciprocate the gesture without falling over. It seemed that even here there was no escape from reminders of Becky's death.

She eased down gratefully into the child pose, idly wishing she could stay curled up with her knees tucked under her forever. Life would be so much simpler. Beside Paula, Megan Jenkins had also come to join in the exercise. *Long sleeves in this weather*, Victoria thought. *She must be boiling.* Megan glanced furtively at Victoria once or twice as though she was trying to gather up the courage to speak to her.

"And now, lie on your back. Bring your knees up to your chest, and rock gently side to side. Good."

Victoria tried to relax, but she kept seeing Steve's face in front of her, his fury at John.

"That guy loses no opportunity to try to get you away from me," he had exploded later as they'd stood on Janet's front porch.

"It was just a hug," Victoria had objected.

"And you really believe that?" Steve had laughed sardonically. "The guy's a womanizer."

"You're a bit of a womanizer yourself," Victoria had snapped. "Look how you treated Claire."

"I asked her to a dance, Vicky." He shook his head in disbelief. "I didn't swear eternal love or propose to the girl. She knew full well we were just friends."

"Did she?"

"Sure." Steve had looked down at her, and she'd melted inside, her anger dissipating. She had wondered why she'd never noticed what dark eyes he had, so intense and, she'd privately admitted, intriguing, because you were never sure what was going on behind them. He'd put his arms around her and gazed down at her thoughtfully. "We should go away for a bit together. Get away from it all."

She had longed to say yes, but the thought of her sister had made her pause.

"Not until Becky gets the justice she deserves."

"Just a few days," he'd said coaxingly, but she had shaken her head.

"Not right now, Steve."

"And breathe in and out," the yoga instructor said, interrupting Victoria's thoughts. She breathed in, counting slowly, and out. *Eight . . . nine . . . ten. Better.* The throbbing in her temples gradually subsided, and she felt her shoulders relax. She wasn't sure how long she lay there, but a gentle hand on her arm made her open her eyes. Paula Gardner.

Around her, all the others who'd come down to the beach were folding up their towels, chatting to one another. Behind her, she saw Megan lingering for a moment or two and then, when she caught Victoria's eye, taking fright and walking away.

Victoria frowned. "Did I fall asleep?" She blinked and stared up at Paula Gardner.

The retired English schoolteacher nodded in amusement. "*Sleep that knits up the raveled sleave of care,*" Paula quoted, and Victoria groggily rose to her feet. She shook out her towel.

"Shakespeare?" she guessed.

Paula nodded. "They're doing Shakespeare at the Hancock Inn at the end of the month, and I've been helping with the prompting, so I'm indulging my love of both drama and poetry at the same time. You should come watch."

"I heard about it from John. Sounds great." Victoria frowned as Paula's reference to poetry triggered a memory. "There is a poem hanging on the wall of John's surgery," she said.

"'My Last Duchess'," Paula said.

Victoria nodded. "I looked up the poem because it seemed somehow to describe my late sister, and while I was doing the yoga relaxation now, I suddenly remembered an old photo of Becky that reminded me of the duchess in the poem. How she took delight in all that was around her, regardless of the source. She didn't have favorites. She saw the good in everyone and responded to it with kindness."

Paula Gardner stared at her, troubled. "It is not easy for most people to understand that sort of openness to beauty," she replied slowly.

"My mother certainly didn't," Victoria said.

"It could be very dangerous," Paula replied, perturbed.

"For my mother?"

Paula shook her head as she replied.

"I was referring to your sister."

* * *

Still no word from Megan. And why hadn't she gone to the police station with her husband? Wasn't she concerned about her son? Victoria tapped her phone, perplexed, and was so engrossed in her own thoughts that she didn't hear Janet's doorbell ring until it had been pushed twice.

"Megan?" she called, hurrying to the front door and yanking it open in her hurry to get there before Janet, who was busy making hot dogs in the kitchen, while listening to her children bicker over who was guilty of giving Belle the ketchup to eat.

"Oh. Claire," Victoria said, surprised for a moment.

"John asked me to drop off an invoice," Claire said. She held out the paper.

"Of course. Do you want to come in? I was hoping to chat." So much had happened since the previous night that Victoria had almost forgotten Claire was coming. And Joe. "Come through to the back garden," Victoria said, over the escalating shouts of Janet's noisy offspring. "Quieter there."

"I mustn't stay long." Claire sounded as awkward as Victoria felt. The garden was overgrown with pasture rose, flowering dogwood and elderberry, drawing a flurry of robins, brown thrashers, rabbits, and squirrels. Comparing it with her mother's run-down garden, Victoria wondered why Janet's equally overgrown plot felt so different. Maybe happy families somehow projected their atmosphere onto their surroundings, however long it had been since the grass had been cut.

They sat on wrought-iron chairs set on the paved area overlooking the fishpond (the family still called it that, though the last fish had long since expired). Each time Claire shifted her weight, the back foot of her chair lifted an inch or two off the ground, leaving her feeling as though she was about to be launched out into the water.

Victoria inhaled, mustering her courage. "I wanted to say how sorry I am," she rushed in at last. "For the way Steve and I got together. I didn't even think at the time. I know you — cared."

Claire smiled wryly. "He never did though," she said.

"I'm sorry," Victoria repeated.

Claire shook her head. "I'm not angry. Not anymore." she replied. "These things happen. Steve never pretended to be in love with me." Her smile was slightly wistful. "The only person I'm angry with is myself."

"Please don't be." Victoria impulsively stretched out her hand. As Claire took it, she overbalanced in the rickety chair. Unable to right herself, she would have toppled onto the brick paving had an arm not suddenly grabbed her.

"Joe!" Claire exclaimed as he helped her straighten, his arm still steadying her and her hand over his. "How did you get in?"

Victoria couldn't have asked for a better entrance if she had orchestrated it herself.

"The door was unlocked," he replied literally.

"Yes, but what are you doing here?"

Joe, his senses overwhelmed by the closeness of Claire's beauty, pointed at the fishpond.

"Ring-necked d-ducks," he said, staring at the plainly empty pond.

"Where?" asked Claire, bewildered.

Victoria adopted a serious expression. "They must have moved on. I haven't seen them today."

Joe glanced at her, the slightest hint of amusement touching his face. "Right," he said. "Pity."

Claire looked down at her hand and blushing, removed it from his.

"Dinner's ready!" yelled Carrie, tearing through the house as she looked for her father and Victoria. She poked her head out the back door. "Dinner!" she bellowed again, then raced off.

"Janet's making dinner, and she assured me she has enough to feed an army," said Victoria. "You guys in the mood for hot dogs?"

"Sure," said Claire.

Joe gave a shy smile. "L-lead the way."

CHAPTER 31

Hancock Inn was abuzz with the excitement of anticipation as almost the whole town seemed to have gathered for *Project Shakespeare*.

"Two shows and dinner," exclaimed Janet in Victoria's ear as they arrived at the inn. Victoria, glancing across to the doorway, noticed Megan Jenkins standing nervously next to it with a glass in one hand. She was about to approach Megan when she saw that a server was helping her mop up her drink, which she had spilled. Later then.

"Where's Steve got to?"

Victoria smoothed her new dress, a summery 1950s-style number, cerise with a scoop neck and a skirt that puffed out from the waist, as she pointed to her right and waved.

"There's my girl," Steve grinned, strolling across and taking her hand. "Do you think anyone will believe we're together when they see you looking like this and I'm still in my old jeans?"

"You are well aware how good you look in your 'old' jeans," Janet said. "Stop fishing for compliments and get your girlfriend a seat."

"Yes, ma'am," he replied. "Let's go, Vicky. You look gorgeous."

Vicky laughed and felt for a moment like a teenager again. "Thanks, Detective McCade," she replied. They found seats a few rows ahead of Claire and Joe.

"Show's starting," Steve said. "*Much Ado About Nothing.*"

"Love it," she whispered to Steve as Beatrice and Benedick clashed and courted across the stage. "'Too wise to woo peaceably.' Is that us?"

Steve flashed her a smile. "I guess so."

When at last the comedy was over, Victoria felt as though she'd been soaring through another world. She sat in a literary daze, tucking into the inn's picnic dinner of fried chicken and salads. The next Shakespeare, *Richard III*, was about to start when a voice spoke in her ear.

"Hello, Victoria."

Victoria jumped up when she saw who it was. "Megan! I've been trying to get hold of you!"

"Could we speak somewhere quieter?" There was an edge to Megan's voice that banished all hesitation from Victoria's answer.

"My car. No one will think of looking for you there."

They slipped out into the dark and hurried to where Victoria had parked.

"You've been wanting to speak to me about Maurice," Victoria invited her once they were seated inside. "And maybe Gavin?"

Megan didn't respond to the second question, other than to shrink back against the car seat as though she was scared Victoria's voice would carry across to the theater. "Did I tell you Maurice has business interests in Chicago?" she asked.

"I live there."

"You're not the only one," Megan muttered. "Maurice was very involved in an import–export company there and spent several months a year in Chicago at one stage. There were — irregularities. Money going missing."

A vague sense of *déjà vu* rippled through Victoria's mind, leaving behind only the disturbed sense of an elusive memory.

"Tell me more."

"Maurice told me the culprit had been discovered. A woman, he said. I was here in Hancock, so everything I heard was secondhand. Apparently, Maurice said the woman was in real trouble though. She claimed innocence. Said she'd been framed. Even accused the company of sending someone to intimidate her. She alleged someone had once almost throttled her when she'd stayed to work late. The only way her assailant could have got into the building would have been if he had been working there or if someone had let him in."

"And you didn't believe her?"

"Why would I have? I had never even met her or her family."

"But you have doubts now? Why?"

Megan turned to face Victoria. "Gavin has always been someone who questioned everything and everyone, including his father. Especially his father. After he told me he thought Maurice had been pursuing Rebecca, he became even more rebellious than usual, especially when I took Maurice's side."

"What form did his rebellion take?"

"He would disappear for hours at a time. Not tell us where he'd been. Several times, I found him in Maurice's office on his computer. Thankfully, Maurice never did."

Megan's hands half rose to the scarf around her neck and then fell. "And then you came here, and Gavin started up with the whole story of Rebecca and my husband again. I told him it was nonsense. Supported Maurice's decision to send him to therapy." Megan stared down at the dark floor. "And then you were attacked at Norway Pond. Throttled."

"Like the woman in Chicago," Victoria said.

Megan nodded. "Like her. And Gavin started talking to me again. Said he'd been spending time with the new vet, John Gardner. Apparently he moved here fairly recently."

"From Chicago," said Victoria, a sick sensation in her stomach. "His wife died."

"You didn't wonder what made him choose Hancock?" Megan asked, her eyes strained.

Victoria felt as though the sound of her pounding heart filled the car. "Are you telling me the woman at Maurice's company in Chicago—?"

"Was Gina. John's wife."

"And John came here because— but surely not?"

Megan nodded.

"He came to find out who was behind the financial embezzlement that led ultimately to his wife's death. He and Gavin have been piecing together what they know for some time now."

Victoria felt dizzy, though whether from pent-up excitement or disbelief, she couldn't tell.

"The attack on you was too similar to the one on John's wife for them to ignore."

"You confronted Maurice?"

"I couldn't believe that someone I loved and trusted so — wholeheartedly — could be someone I didn't know at all. But finally, yes, I confronted him. I don't know what Maurice told you when he went to the police station, but Gavin accused him. Maurice lost his cool and threw Gavin out, and he hasn't returned. And when Gavin walked out, something inside me snapped. For once, I chose the part of my son."

"Where is Gavin now?"

Megan shook her head, her eyes swimming. "I don't know. I can't sleep at night worrying about him. Maurice is livid and desperate to find him in case he goes to the police."

"And what do you think of Gavin's accusations? Is he a liar as his father says?"

"He's telling the truth."

"You think it was Maurice who attacked me?"

Smiling unhappily, Megan rolled up her sleeves and pulled down her scarf. She pointed to her arms and neck. Even in the dim light, they were vivid with purple and black bruises.

"Before I stood up to him, I suspected it might be Maurice," she said simply. "Now I know."

* * *

"We have our killer then," exclaimed Steve the next morning to Karen and Victoria. "The guy is violent and always gets his own way. When Rebecca kept rejecting Maurice, he finally snapped and killed her. Or maybe John told her about Maurice's business activities, and she threatened to go to the police."

"What about the forensic results?" Karen's tone was harsher than usual. No doubt she was thinking of Claire and how hard she had taken Steve's rejection. Victoria found herself hoping again that Joe would be able to console Claire. If only he weren't so nervous, compared to Steve's abundant confidence.

"They say that Rebecca's killer was different from Victoria's assailant," Karen continued.

"He probably hired someone to kill her," Steve said. "Like he presumably hired Todd to take the warning message to Victoria. The guy uses people. Just like he uses women."

"Women are people too," Karen said curtly, and Victoria knew she was thinking of Claire again. Steve shot her a glance but seemed to decide it wiser not to respond.

"We need to find Gavin. I'll start with John," Victoria said. "Probably too obvious a hiding place to be likely, but maybe he'll have some idea as to who Gavin could be with." She clicked her tongue. "I have a few questions for him too. I always thought he was hiding something."

"I'll take care of Dr Gardner," said Steve, his lips tightening. "I don't trust him with you."

"Please, no," said Victoria, closing her eyes. "All we need is for the police to be in the news for roughing up the local vet. You know you're itching to put those kickboxing moves into practice."

"I'll go with you to see him," Karen told Victoria. "I need to drop off Claire's house keys for her anyway. When she hurried out this morning, she forgot them. Again. Goodness knows how she'll manage without me when I finally get her to leave home!"

"Look after yourself then." Steve took Victoria's hand and bent to give her a swift kiss while Karen's back was turned. "I'll come by Janet's this evening — I'm taking you out for dinner tonight." He kissed her again.

Victoria blushed and squeezed his hand.

"No office canoodling!" exclaimed Karen, turning around. "You're putting me off my lunch. Come on, let's go!"

When Karen and Victoria got to the surgery, the only other person in the waiting room was Joe.

Karen stared at the young man. "What are you doing here?"

Joe paused, then spoke in a rush as though racing to get the words out before his stammer tripped him. "I've just got a cat." He pointed to a bedraggled feline in a basket that glared at Joe ferociously.

"He looks wild," Karen said.

"A little," Joe acknowledged. "Feral. Todd used t-to feed him. I f-found him crying outside the Harris Center about a week ago and took over."

"He looks like he needs a lot of medical attention," Victoria said, even more doubtfully than Karen, staring at the cat's bitten ear and patchy skin. "How often has he been to the vet?"

Joe blushed. "Almost every d-day."

"Where is John?" demanded Victoria.

"I'm here." John strolled in from the operating room and groaned as he saw Joe. "Is Fluffy back?" he said, receiving a malevolent glare from the indignant feline.

"Fluffy can wait," said Karen. "John, can we chat to you? And where's Claire? She forgot her keys."

"She's at the back, feeding the animals who stayed overnight," said John. "Perhaps Joe can take the keys to her for you if you want to talk? Vicky, Karen, shall we go through? What's up?" He escorted them to his office.

Victoria took the seat opposite him. "Any idea where Gavin Jenkins is?"

"Why? Who's looking for Gavin?"

"Just about everyone," said Karen. "His father. Steve. Victoria. Me. We thought you might know where he was."

"Why would I?" asked John, his expression blank.

"Cut the act, John," Vicky said. "Megan told me everything."

John froze. "What is *everything*?" he said slowly.

"I know why you moved to Hancock," Vicky replied. "You came to find out who framed Gina. It's time you started being honest with me."

"I've always been honest with you," John replied. "But I'm not required to tell you everything about my past."

"So you did come here to see if you could nail Maurice?"

John didn't answer for a moment.

"He as good as killed her, Vicky," he said quietly. "She lived in constant fear. She was intimidated, assaulted at work, by him or someone connected to him. Accused of embezzlement. And he got away with it."

"Until now," Karen replied. "What do you have on him?"

"Gavin has been gathering information on him," John answered. "He's a whizz with technology, and I contacted a few friends who worked with Gina to help us get access to their system. I don't know where he is though."

"Let's talk about Becky, then," said Victoria. "Anything you've been hiding about your friendship with her? Why did you phone Becky so often, John, if you were only friends?"

John looked at her for a moment as though trying to decide whether to speak. "I was trying to protect her. She was being harassed."

St. Patrick wandered in and sniffed at Victoria then laid his head on her knee. She stroked his ears. "Harassed? You mean Maurice?"

John nodded. "He kept trying to see her. At first during work and then when she refused to, he started coming to her house. Bringing her unwanted presents. He wouldn't take no for an answer. When Steve and I got into a fight at her house, it was because I thought he was Maurice."

"That's what Gavin said."

"She was terrified of him. But she didn't want to get the police involved. She made me promise not to. So I offered to phone her each evening to check she made it home safely."

"And there was never more to your relationship?"

"Nope. Not from her side. In fact, I began wondering if she was seeing someone, because the last week or so, she didn't always answer her calls, or she phoned me back later. Once she answered, and I heard a guy's voice in the background. Who knows? I asked her if she wanted me to stop calling, but she said she felt safer knowing she had a friend who was looking out for her. That she trusted me."

"And you kept hoping she'd stop seeing you as just a friend?" Victoria suggested.

"Yeah. Stupid, huh?"

Victoria smiled back at him. "I guess we're all stupid when it comes to love."

* * *

"So, where are you taking me?" Victoria asked Steve as they left Janet's home that evening.

"How do you feel about Italian?" he asked, reversing the Tesla into the street. "I know a place just outside Hancock along the Contoocook River."

"I'll never say no. I can't remember the last time I had pasta. Or piccata. Or—" she coughed. "I'll stop there."

"Piccata it is then. Didn't eat out a lot in Chicago, did you?"

"Well, I often got takeaways for myself. Chinese or pizza usually or — no, I didn't," she admitted, adding hastily, "work kept me very busy."

Steve smiled but didn't answer, his eyes on the road.

"It's still light," he said. "I made a reservation, but we could get takeaways and have a picnic outdoors somewhere?"

Victoria's mind flashed back to the late-night meals, eaten out of cardboard boxes on her bed, in Morgan Park.

"I'm going with the restaurant."

As they pulled up to the double-story restaurant, its white balcony overlooking green lawns, Victoria's smile faded at the sight of a familiar, rather battered green Chevrolet Spark.

She ducked her head down as she climbed out the car and slammed the passenger door shut.

"Hey, Vicky, someone's waving to you," Steve called.

Victoria sighed as she looked up, knowing already who she would see. Steve frowned at the woman, her unruly gray hair framing a gentle face and faded eyes of cornflower blue, as she climbed out of the Spark.

"Isn't that your mother's friend?"

"It is," Victoria said grimly.

"Vicky!" the woman exclaimed. She smiled at Steve. "Evening, Detective McCade."

Steve smiled and took Victoria's hand. Victoria groaned inwardly, hoping her mother's friend hadn't noticed, and pulled her fingers from Steve's.

"Sybil," Victoria replied, trying to sound enthusiastic. "I thought you were on holiday."

"Just a few days," she replied. "How are you, dear? We saw you far too briefly the other day at the concert. I was so sorry to hear from your mother that you couldn't make Becky's memorial."

"How is my mother?" Vicky asked to change the subject.

"You haven't seen her recently?" Sybil asked in mild surprise. "I've only visited her once or twice since I got back, but she isn't all that well."

"When is she ever?" Victoria said under her breath. She managed a faint smile. "Are you meeting someone for dinner?"

"A friend of mine."

"We're not staying," Victoria said quickly. "Just getting takeaways, right, Steve?" She nudged him so he'd play along. "It's been a busy day at work for us both." She tried to make it sound like they were just colleagues who happened to be dropping in to pick up a meal.

"Right," Steve agreed readily, putting his arm around Victoria and kissing the top of her head. *No possibility of missing that,* Victoria thought as she watched Sybil's eyes widening.

A silver Fiat drew up. "I think that's your friend?" Victoria said hopefully.

"Yes, I'd better go. Enjoy your meal, and I'll let your mother know I've seen you."

"I bet that's the first thing she'll do," Victoria muttered a few moments later, as they walked toward the restaurant. "She probably won't even wait till she sees her to pass on the news."

They placed their order, then returned to the car to wait. "You sure you're happy with pizza again after all those Chicago takeaways? You really didn't want to eat the long-awaited piccata in style inside?" Steve suggested.

"No, no," Victoria sighed. "Sybil's spoiled my appetite. I don't want to sit in the restaurant with her watching us. She's probably sending my mother a text right now."

"Or there's sausage casserole. You could still change your mind?" Steve was reading the menu off his phone.

"No! My mother will explode when she hears! Won't she?"

"I expect so," Steve replied lightly.

Victoria's eyes narrowed.

"You're glad, aren't you?"

"What?"

Steve's phone rang.

"Our food is ready! Shall I go, or do you want to?"

Victoria shook her head.

She watched Steve as he jogged toward the restaurant entrance.

"One pizza coming up!" he exclaimed a few minutes later. "Only a pleasure," he added, in response to Victoria's silence.

"You did it deliberately."

"Bought you pizza? I plead guilty."

"Don't play dumb. You wanted Sybil to find out we're together. You know my mother doesn't like you, and she's going to be livid, and you're pleased."

Steve's smile faded.

"Let's head home," he said shortly, shoving their takeaways on the seat behind him.

They drove in silence the short distance back to Hancock. To Victoria, it felt like an eternity.

"Enjoy the pizza." Steve dumped the box onto her lap as Janet's front garden came into view.

"Steve, wait." Victoria felt close to tears. "Let's go back to your place for a while. Chat a bit."

"What is there to say?"

"I'm sorry?" Victoria suggested.

He nodded curtly.

"I can't talk for long. I have an early start tomorrow," he said as they pulled up at his place.

Victoria followed him silently up the pathway to his door. He switched on the light and gestured to the couch.

She sat down, her body sinking onto the soothing coolness of the black leather, her pizza beside her.

"Look, I overreacted," she began, her voice wavering. "I felt you were taking pleasure in the whole situation because it's going to drive my mother mad."

Steve took a deep breath, his eyes locked on hers, intense and inscrutable. Then, instead of sitting on the couch, he went down on his haunches before her and slowly withdrew her hands from where they were nervously clasped behind her knees, and held them.

"I felt as though you were ashamed of being seen with me," he said. "Like you think I'm not good enough for your mother."

Her fingers tightened over his.

"You did? You really thought that?"

"Yeah. I was trying to brush it off so you wouldn't see I was—"

"Hurt?"

Steve nodded.

"Steve, I'm so sorry," she whispered. "I would never think that. You're way too good for a messed-up family like ours. My mother has never been there for me when I needed her. But you — you walked me to my car at the hospital to make sure I was safe, you sat through a whole Shakespeare romcom with me, you planned our dinner tonight and made a reservation and everything—" She sniffed and removed her hand from his to rummage in her pocket for a handkerchief. "I know *you* are there for me. That I can trust you."

He gave the skew smile that made her throat go dry.

"Hey," he whispered caressingly.

"Yes?"

"Your pizza isn't going to taste any better if it's wet." He grinned, wiping her eyes with a napkin from the pizza box.

She laughed and kissed him. His fingers tightened over hers as he kissed her back. The pizza was forgotten.

* * *

Victoria steeled herself to go through her mother's front door. It was standing ajar, and the hallway was dark.

"Mother? I got your message."

A faint reply came from the bedroom, and Victoria stumbled through, tripping over an umbrella that was strewn across the floor.

Her mother was in bed, staring out at a sliver of light showing through the heavy curtains.

"And so I hear you are with Steve McCade. You never learn, do you? Leave him, Vicky. He's no good. Do you understand me?"

Victoria had never heard her mother's voice quite so full of loathing.

"You need to leave him."

Victoria shook her head. "I'm not leaving him."

Vera twisted her neck slightly to look over her shoulder at her daughter, her eyes wide. "You always make bad choices when it comes to men. You know me, my child. I have to speak my mind. I've always been a very plain speaker."

There wasn't even a hint of irony in her voice.

Victoria felt too tired even for anger. She went across to where her mother was lying and sat down on the edge of the bed beside her.

"And you didn't make a bad choice? Tell me something." Victoria paused, trying to decide how to lead up to what she wanted to ask. "Are you absolutely sure that Becky had no one in her life?"

Vera's eyes slid up to Victoria's and then shifted away. "There was no one. Becky knew that men were not to be trusted."

Victoria was sure her mother was lying. "Men like my father?"

Vera glanced at her daughter once more, her face white. "Like your father," she repeated, her eyes focusing on some faraway memory. Victoria thought it was the closest to an admission that her mother had ever come — except that she got the sense Vera was not referring to her father's abuse.

"What did my father do *to you* to make you distrust him?" Victoria probed gently.

"He—"

For a moment, Vicky thought her mother was going to tell her.

"I don't know what you are talking about," she replied tiredly. "All I know is that you abandoned us. If you had been here, Becky wouldn't have died. You would have protected her."

"Like you never did?" snapped Victoria.

"You should have been here!" Vera lifted herself up, her dull, dry voice rising to a shriek of fury. "You abandoned us for Chicago."

"The worst I ever did was want a life of my own!" Victoria shouted back. "And it's what I wanted for Becky too."

Vera collapsed down onto the pillows, her chest rising and falling, like a sparrow that had flown into a windowpane. A thin-lipped smile revealed the lines etched in the brittle skin around her mouth. "Becky wasn't like you," she whispered. "She valued family."

"And if she had decided she wanted more than this?" demanded Victoria, her arm sweeping across the cluttered, crowded heaviness of the dark room. "Would you have tried to stop her?"

Vera turned away so that her daughter couldn't see her expression. "I only ever wanted what was best for her." She swiveled around suddenly, her features quivering, though whether from anger or some other emotion, Vicky could not tell. "And I knew what was best for her. I *did*. Didn't I?"

"Did you?" muttered Victoria. She stared at her mother, but the older woman wouldn't meet her eyes.

Victoria shook her head, perplexed. *What do you know about my father that you aren't telling me? What do you know about Becky that you won't share?*

She bit her lip. Maybe her mother was right. Perhaps she should have been here. Maybe she could have saved her sister. The thought was agonizing.

"I've got to go," she said finally. The house and all its memories felt like they were closing in on her. "I've got to go."

CHAPTER 32

"You know Gavin and Megan Jenkins slightly, don't you?" Victoria asked Janet. "Any idea where he might be hiding out? What are his interests?"

Janet shook her head, then her face lit up. "I seem to remember Megan saying he liked animals. Hiking. The outdoors. What about the Harris Center if he's keen on wildlife? I think he occasionally helped Joe with his research."

"Good idea. I'll get in contact with Joe. It's Wednesday, so he and John should be there. I'll give them a ring and head off there now. You want me to take the kids along to give you a break?"

"Please! Blake's still on leave, and I never get a moment alone with him with these two around," said Janet, grabbing Carrie and kissing her on the forehead.

Victoria regretted her offer the second she pulled up at the Harris Center building.

"Hey, look at this," called Harvey. He leaped out of the car and swooped his toy airplane down with his arm, almost knocking over an elderly lady returning from a gentle stroll.

Victoria cringed. "Sorry. Carrie, don't pick the flowers please! Come on, guys. You need to behave now. This building is very special and has been carefully designed using lots of recycled or natural materials. And look — they even have solar panels to make electricity."

"I want to play outside! I don't *want* to go in!" moaned Harvey. "I don't want to talk to Joe now."

"Hey, Carrie! Hi, Harvey!" called a voice, and they turned to see John coming down the steps. "You guys want to play out here with St. Patrick while Victoria chats to Joe?"

"Yeah!" Carrie and Harvey raced across to St. Patrick. He stood solidly, wagging his tail, as they flung their arms around him.

John sat down on the steps of the building. "I'll watch them," he offered. "Joe's inside."

Victoria hurried off, eager to find Joe, who rose immediately when he saw her.

"You thought I c-could help you with Gavin?" he asked.

"Seeing Gavin is a wildlife fan, we thought you might be able to suggest someone connected to the Harris Center who might have given him somewhere to stay."

Joe thought for a moment. "I know he was involved in the Hancock Bobcat Den Project."

"There are bobcats here?"

"Yeah. He loved that. And I think he did *shinrin-yoku* a few times."

Victoria blinked. "I beg your pardon?"

"Forest bathing." Joe laughed at her expression. "A f-form of nature therapy. Relaxation exercises. Yoga. Awareness of your surroundings. I'll give you the numbers of those running the bobcat project."

"And the tree-hugging," Victoria added, feeling excited that at last she might have some leads.

"Forest bathing," Joe corrected with a grin. "You should t-try it. Very soothing." He forwarded the contacts to her phone as he spoke. "Good luck. Hope you find him."

She walked outside, blinking in the sunshine and put up her hand to shade her eyes. Where was John? And where, she wondered, her heart sinking, were the children?

She ran down the steps. "Harvey? Carrie?" she called.

To her relief, St. Patrick came bounding toward her, closely followed by John, with Harvey and Carrie trotting behind him.

"Where were you?" Victoria snapped.

Carrie pointed over her shoulder. "I went on that trail."

"She ran off before I could stop her," said John, who was out of breath from the unexpected effort of running after small children.

"It's really cool!" Carrie exclaimed. "You just follow the yellow rectangles, and they show you where to go. And look what I found!" She held up a battered piece of plastic.

"I found one too!" said Harvey, pushing her out of the way.

Victoria turned the bits over in her hand. "Looks like junk."

John looked at her grimly. "Not at all," he said, taking a third piece of plastic from his pocket. "This is the rest of it that they found."

Victoria's hands rose up to her mouth as he passed her the remains of a crushed cell phone.

"You suspect it could be your sister's?" asked John.

Victoria looked at him, confirmation in her eyes.

"It looks like someone heavy stepped on it," piped up Carrie. "It's all broken."

"Yeah." Victoria's voice was unsteady. "It's all broken now."

* * *

Janet knocked on the door of Victoria's bedroom and opened it enough to poke her head around. "Are you hungry?"

Victoria shook her head.

Janet walked in without asking and sat down on the bed where Victoria lay huddled under blankets in spite of the heat of the evening.

"You're going to find him."

"Who?" She knew who Janet was referring to, she just couldn't find the words, the energy, to sit up and talk about him.

"The bastard who killed your sister and destroyed her phone."

"I thought so too," Victoria whispered. She closed her eyes. "I'm so tired."

Janet nodded. "At least you can cross Joe off your list. He only has eyes for Claire. I could have beaned him over the head with his hot dog the other night, and he still wouldn't have stopped gazing at her."

Victoria grinned faintly.

"That was pretty amazing, the way he came through into the garden as if on cue and caught her just in time. I didn't realize how strong he was."

How strong he— She shook her head. He was with Claire when Todd was attacked. He couldn't possibly be a suspect.

Victoria sighed, shaking her head. "I find myself questioning everyone."

Janet grinned. "As long as you don't suspect me, we're okay."

Victoria reached out impulsively. "I would never suspect you, Janet," she said. "You are one of the few people that I truly trust."

CHAPTER 33

"Victoria!"

Someone was calling her, but strong hands were choking her and forcing her head under water. She clawed at the merciless fingers, trying to break free.

The harder she fought, the further she was submerged. Nothing made a difference. Her lungs were on fire, and for a moment, she went limp, ready to give in. Then the voice came again.

"Victoria!"

Someone needed her. The voice triggered an unexpected surge of strength, and she gripped her assailant's wrists and yanked her head backwards as hard as she could. Relief flooded her as the suffocating fingers lost their grasp.

"*Victoria*!"

She woke with a jolt, her breaths coming in noisy gasps, her heart pounding. Her hands massaged her neck subconsciously.

There was a knock at her window. She swung around and saw a face peering through the pane in the morning light.

"What on earth — Gavin?"

She leaped out of bed and hurried to open the window. Victoria hauled the grubby teen in and stared at him, wondering for a moment if he was still part of her nightmare. "Where have you been? We've been looking everywhere for you. Your mother's been worried sick."

"Yeah, hiding out in the woods by the Harris Center," he said, apparently unconcerned about his mother. "Roughing it."

"Hugging trees?" Victoria asked sardonically.

"What? Listen, Victoria, I ran away because I was scared. Of my dad. He is in it up to here in shady business deals. I have proof. I hacked into his accounts on my laptop." He handed her a flash drive. "It's all there."

"All there?" Victoria thought for a moment about John and swallowed back the lump in her throat. Then she turned to the boy. "You'd better phone your mother," she said with a forced smile. She reached for a light sweater and pulled it on. "Ask Janet to let you use her phone. And clean yourself up."

"Where are you going?" Gavin demanded, responding to Victoria's second instruction by pulling a couple of leaves out of his hair and dropping them carelessly on the carpet.

"Out!" she replied over her shoulder.

* * *

Victoria stormed into John's surgery. "I've found Gavin!"

John looked up quickly from the file he was reading. "And?"

Victoria passed him the flash drive. "The info on here is enough to jail Maurice for years."

John was silent for a moment. He took her hand and held it lightly, an inarticulate expression of gratitude where words would have been inadequate. "Thank you," he said at last.

* * *

Janet flopped down onto the worn couch in her living room and beckoned to Victoria. "Alcohol," she said. "I need alcohol."

Victoria grinned and brought through the tray from the kitchen. "Two champagnes coming up. We're celebrating.

Maurice has been arrested and John's wife vindicated. I've been given the rest of the day off as a reward."

Janet looked at her and held up a badly misshapen spoon, the plastic twisted almost out of recognition and covered in what looked like bite marks.

"*You* are celebrating," she said. "I am recovering. Belle has destroyed my serving spoon, eaten half the cold stew I was going to heat up for dinner, and annihilated my very expensive sunglasses. If Blake and the kids hadn't taken her out for a walk, I would have murdered her."

Victoria felt her phone vibrating in her pocket and fumbled for it. "Hold that thought." She accepted the call from an unknown number.

"Detective Wharton?"

Victoria listened intently as the voice on the other end spoke briefly. "Yes, yes, any time," she replied. "Day or night." She ended the call and stared at Janet. "It was the hospital. Apparently, they've been trying to get hold of me all day. They kept getting Steve on the phone at the police station. Wanted to tell me that Todd has regained consciousness and is asking for me. He's asleep again, but they'll phone as soon as he wakes. They finally reached Karen, who gave them my cell number."

Janet frowned. "Why didn't Steve let you know?"

Victoria shook her head, unable to think of an answer. She pulled up his number. "Engaged," she replied. She waited, tried once more, then shoved her phone back in her pocket. "No answer."

Janet shrugged. "He'll probably explain when you see him. You'd better let your mother know that you may finally have answers. If Todd can tell you who attacked him, you should also have Becky's killer."

Victoria groaned. "Yeah, you're right," she admitted. "I'll head over that way now. Maybe stop first at the police station to see if I can find Steve and ask him what's going on."

Janet looked up with wide, pleading eyes. "Can I finish off your champagne?"

Victoria grinned and handed her the glass.

CHAPTER 34

When Vicky got to the police station, only Karen was there. "Any idea where Steve is?" she asked.

Karen shook her head. "Any more leads on the phone you found?" she asked Victoria.

Victoria sighed. "Yeah. It's my sister's. As we assumed."

Karen placed a hand on her shoulder. "I'm sorry," she said simply.

Victoria nodded, unable to speak.

"I'm heading out," Karen said, "Will you be okay?"

"Sure."

Victoria stared blankly into space for a moment, listening to Karen's footsteps recede.

Where are Becky's phone records? she thought suddenly. She hurried across to Steve's computer and opened it.

"Password, password," she muttered. She called Steve's number. Unavailable again. Victoria slammed down her phone and stared at the laptop.

Knowing she shouldn't, she tentatively typed in Steve's name into the password bar. Incorrect. She tried his surname — incorrect. On an impulse, she typed in "Victoria." Incorrect. Victoria breathed out a sigh, then tensed again. There was something else she could try.

She held her breath as she pushed enter, not sure whether to pray it worked or to pray that it didn't.

She closed her eyes for a moment, then opened them to see his desktop home screen appear. Her heart sank.

His password was *Becky*.

Numbly, she opened his email, and when that showed nothing, searched through all likely folders.

"Where are they?" She sighed in frustration, closed the last document and returned to the desktop. She saw an unnamed folder and opened it, guilt and trepidation crawling in her stomach. A list of photograph files, all unnamed like the folder, came up. She opened the first one and stared at the laughing girl in the picture.

"Becky," she said. She opened more photos. Becky laughing with friends. Becky with her arms around Steve. Another one of her kissing Steve. Becky helping out at a church sale. Becky pulling a face and clowning around with John, a slightly fuzzy picture as though taken without their knowing. Unbidden, lines from 'My Last Duchess' flashed into Victoria's mind:

That's my last Duchess painted on the wall . . .
. . . she smiled, no doubt,
Whene'er I passed her; but who passed without
Much the same smile?

She no longer needed the phone records, she realized. The photographs told her what the records would reveal.

There was one last unopened photo file she hadn't seen. She braced herself to see Becky's smiling face once more. She double-clicked. Her hand rose to her mouth.

A sick feeling swam inside her as she stared at the familiar lines around the eyes, the thin lips smiling back at her.

"Dad?" she whispered.

* * *

John knocked on the open door of the police station. When no one answered, he walked in to find Victoria gazing unseeingly out of the window. He tapped her on the shoulder. Victoria jumped and swung around.

"Woah! It's me! I just came to let you know my mom says she's so grateful for all you did for Gina." John put out a flat palm against the fist Victoria had raised against him. Victoria stared at John for a moment, her hand still clenched.

"Sit down," John said. "You're shaking."

Victoria shook her head. "I have to go to my mother. As soon as Karen is back at the station."

"You shouldn't be going anywhere." John scratched his head.

"Don't try to stop me."

John grinned. "I'd be too scared to," he said, nodding at her fist. He slowly took her hand and unclenched it. "I'll walk there with you," he offered. "I won't come inside."

By the time Karen had returned, Victoria had almost stopped trembling.

"Adrenaline," she muttered, holding her outstretched hands before her for inspection. She nodded at John. "We'd better be on our way."

They left the building. "What's going on?" John asked.

"I found a photo of my father on Steve's computer."

"That's disturbing." John frowned. "How did you find it?"

"I wanted my sister's phone records and hacked into his computer when he kept delaying giving them to me. His password was *Becky*," she said. "He has photos of her too. They were obviously together."

John grimaced. "Yeah, I suspected so. Especially when we got into a fight outside her place."

"And you didn't say anything?"

John shrugged. "I assumed you guessed too."

"Yes, all the signs were there." Victoria sighed. "His calling her Becky, not giving me the phone records. His jealousy of you. What bothers me the most is that he never told me."

"You want to admit why that frightens you so much?" John asked. "Saying it aloud doesn't necessarily make your suspicions true."

Victoria fought to stop her voice from choking. "We're almost here," she said, her mother's neglected garden coming into sight.

She glanced up at John. "You're right," she admitted. "I'm terrified that the real reason Steve said nothing was—"

At that moment, her phone rang. She swiped her screen to accept the call. "Todd?"

She hurried up to the house. The door stood ajar.

"Want me to wait for you?" called John, but she didn't hear him. She was listening to the rasping voice on the other end of her phone. She walked into her mother's lounge and her face turned ashen. Vera was not alone.

Victoria ended the call and pointed at the tall man standing by the window, a familiar holster on his hip.

"It was *you*!" she hissed. "You killed my sister!"

Steve turned slowly, his face almost as pale as hers.

"That was Todd on the phone," she said. "He told me everything. How he saw you leaning over my sister's body when you dumped it, how he didn't recognize you until he was arrested and he realized that the man who gave him the threatening note for me was the same man who had killed Becky."

"Don't be ridiculous," Steve scoffed. "Why would he suddenly recognize me then and not before?"

"His eyesight is bad, but his hearing isn't," she replied. "He recognized your voice."

"And you believe him?" Steve replied. A faint smile crossed his face. "A pathetic alcoholic."

"So you didn't offer Todd blackmail money and attack him behind the Meeting House? You mean you didn't try to kill him in the hospital?"

"He told you that?" Steve asked, a smile still playing around his lips.

"He was very lucid," Victoria said through gritted teeth. "Now I know why he was so agitated when he saw us in the hospital and why he kept saying 'Eve'. He was trying to say *your name* and to reveal the murderer." She laughed shortly.

"He also told me that I was right in suspecting you of police brutality — that you hit him at the police station on the evening he was arrested to make him cooperate."

Steve laughed, and Vera stared from her daughter to Steve and back again, her hands opening and closing repeatedly in her lap.

"So you think you have tied up all the loose ends?" Steve said. He came closer and loomed over her. "Maybe I offered Todd money, but you have a far more practiced blackmailer in the woman sitting beside you."

"Be quiet!" Vera interposed, but Steve took no notice.

"Do you want to tell her, Vera, or shall I?"

"Mom, what is he talking about?" Victoria asked, bewildered.

Vera chose her words carefully. "Simply that I decided to take pity on him when he was young and to pay for his studies even though I had very little left after the divorce. If you call that blackmail . . ."

"Why would you do that?" Victoria asked. "You hated him even then."

"Do you want to tell her?" Steve shouted. "About the affair your husband had, a few years after you married?"

Victoria felt nauseous and sat down suddenly.

"Mom, is this true? Who did my father have a relationship with?" she asked, her throat dry.

Steve answered for her.

"My mother," he said.

The nausea now was overwhelming. "Are you saying—?"

Steve nodded. "When I was little, I was left alone at home for hours on end while my mother was out drinking, always trying to find the next man to fulfil the emptiness left by my father. Your father."

"Mom, tell me it's not true," Victoria whispered, but Vera was silent.

"I came to Hancock as a young man," said Steve, "to find the father I had never had, whose absence robbed me of the home life I always wanted."

"So you befriended us — Becky and me — to try to find your father?" asked Victoria.

"Why else?" sneered Steve. "When I discovered he was gone, I confronted Vera. She told me my mother had written to her telling her about my birth, but she had hidden it from my father. She offered to pay for my studies if I would go away."

"He threatened to tell everyone," Vera panted, her voice rising. "Especially you and Becky. To humiliate our family."

"So that was why you left," Victoria said. "You got your money. What made you come back? Wasn't the money enough?"

Steve laughed. "Not even close," he replied. "It was enough to keep me quiet while I studied, but after that . . . your mother robbed me of a father. And then thought it was sufficient to compensate me with cash. She could have told him about me, but she said nothing. And so I came back once I was qualified, this time determined to take revenge."

"You are evil," Vera muttered. "You deliberately started a relationship with Becky to destroy this family. Your own half-sister."

"How could you?" Victoria seethed. "Using Becky like that when you didn't even care for her."

Steve shook his head. "That's where you are wrong," he muttered. "It was something I never could have imagined would happen. I fell for her. She was so beautiful." His voice caught as he spoke of her. "I would have done anything for her. Safeguarded her from Maurice — but she still turned to John for protection. He was always phoning her."

"Maybe she felt safer turning to John than someone who would have beaten Maurice to a pulp the way you did to Joe," Victoria said.

"She did," said Steve in a low voice. "I realize that now."

"Is that why you killed her?" Victoria asked. "Was it jealousy? And what about me? Did you start a relationship with me out of revenge or to distract me from finding out who my sister's murderer was?"

Steve shrugged. "Mostly to distract you," he said, his eyes locked on Victoria's in a cruel, hard stare. "I tried sending Todd with a note too — I knew how poor his eyesight was, so I spoke to him when it was dark and hid my face. But I never really thought threats would be as effective as a relationship. You were so pathetically lonely that I knew from the start you'd be easy prey."

"You're not quite as irresistible as you thought, or we wouldn't be standing here," Victoria answered, struggling to keep away the tears. "And you haven't answered my question. Was it jealousy that made you murder my sister?"

"I didn't murder her," Steve said, his fingers traveling subconsciously to his holster. "I loved her."

"Love! She was your sister! Mom, why didn't you stop them?" Victoria cried, turning to her mother.

"I tried," her mother replied. "I was livid. I confronted Becky and commanded her to end the relationship."

Something in Vera's words made Victoria freeze.

"Say that again," she said.

"What?" Vera held her gaze. "I commanded her to stop."

Victoria swallowed.

"*I gave commands; Then all smiles stopped together.*" she quoted. "From 'My Last Duchess'."

She moved unsteadily toward her mother. "It was you," she whispered. "Wasn't it?"

Vera's face seemed to crack.

"I didn't mean to." Her voice was barely audible. "We had never fought. Becky always listened to me. Until him." She pointed an accusing finger at Steve. "She refused to give him up, and I couldn't tell her why. It would have broken her. Destroyed her. Destroyed our family."

Victoria knelt beside her mother, her hands grasping the wheelchair. "Our family is already so broken. What difference would revealing the truth have made?"

Vera shook her head tiredly. "She and Steve came here to tell me about their relationship. At Steve's insistence, of course. I can still see him standing over there, lounging beside her, one hand in his pocket, the other around a drink. He put down the bottle on the table next to me, pulled her closer, kissing her. He wanted to see how far he could push me."

Vera gave a shuddering sigh. "I begged Becky to leave him. Then I ordered her. When she wouldn't listen, I grabbed her by her arms and shook her. She pulled away, lost her balance, and fell onto her knees next to me. And still she refused to leave him. I was so beside myself that I didn't know what I was doing. Something just — snapped. I snatched up the bottle from the table, and I—"

She sank her head into her hands. "I told Steve I would destroy his career, tell his superiors about his blackmailing and his incestuous relationship if he didn't help me. He took Becky's body and dumped it on one of the trails, but he had forgotten about her phone. His calls and their chat history would incriminate him and make him a suspect. When Paula found Becky, he managed to get a moment alone and crushed the phone and threw it into the bush. It was a stupid thing to do."

"Not as stupid as killing her," hissed Steve, his hand still on his holster. A menacing silence hung in the air. "When I heard that Todd was awake, I came at once to tell Vera we were in trouble."

Victoria suddenly remembered John outside and raised her voice as much as she could without sounding unnatural. "Don't do it, Steve," Victoria ordered. "Drop your hand."

"You know too much," he muttered. "I've worked too hard to get where I am to have you destroy it all. Todd can be bought off. Once he knows you are dead—"

"Mom?" Victoria pleaded. "Say something. Stop him!"

Vera looked away, unable to meet her eyes.

As Steve lifted his gun from the holster, his usual steely calm faltered for a second. His fingers fumbled, and the gun fell.

Victoria made a dart for the weapon at the same time he did, and they grappled wildly on the floor. Her fingers closed over the gun for a moment before Steve snatched it from her hold and rose to his knees, pulling Victoria up with him. She struck out with the heel of her hand to his chin, trying to break free of his hold. He jerked back, but his grip didn't loosen.

"Victoria!"

Steve swung around to see John charging toward them, and Victoria took her chance and wrenched free, snatching for the gun. Her hands closed around Steve's as his finger felt for the trigger. She tried in vain to divert the direction of the weapon, but his hand mercilessly forced the barrel toward her head. Desperate, she dropped her hands and threw herself against him with the full force of her body, knocking him off balance as his finger found the trigger. A shot sounded, and Vera's head sank onto her chest.

Everything swam in slow motion then. Victoria was dimly aware of John wrestling the gun from Steve's hold and pinning him down. Her fingers, clumsy and trembling, felt for her mother's pulse, her heartbeat, anything, and then were still. Nothing. She sank down beside Vera's wheelchair and sobbed.

CHAPTER 35

Norway Pond at sunset no longer held any terror for her. The sand felt soft under her bare feet, and the air was still warm in the twilight. Her fingers clasped a small container carefully as she made her way across the beach. As compact as the container was, she felt the whole weight of her past lay within that small box holding her mother's ashes.

"Victoria."

She glanced up to see John approaching.

"Thank you for coming," she said, taking a deep breath, her fingers tightening over the box. "I've been dreading this day for ages. Not being alone somehow makes it much easier."

"I'm glad you're still here," he replied. "Every time we message or meet up, I expect you're going to tell me you're leaving Hancock." He smiled awkwardly. "Case is over. Steve in jail."

Victoria hesitated a moment before answering.

"It's really just wrapping up my mother's estate that I still need to sort out. Of course, it's been busy at the police station too."

"Poor Karen," John nodded. "She's lucky you were there to help out the last while."

"Yes, after Steve's arrest, she begged me to stay and help her in his place — I was planning to continue just until the case was finished," Victoria replied, "but she was so overwhelmed with work that she asked me to carry on until she had a chance to breathe or until someone was appointed to assist her. Things seem to be quietening down now," she added.

"Oh. Right. That's good. I suppose."

"I suppose." Victoria paused. "It gives me more time to help out Janet around the house now that there's another baby on the way. It's the best way I can pay her back for putting me up for so long. It's pretty crazy and messy there most of the time, but it's nice crazy. But I can't stay there forever, especially now."

John nodded, his eyes far away for a moment as though lingering on a past memory.

"Yes, they'll need the extra space," he said at last. "Everyone seems to be moving on. Even Claire's left home."

"She showed me her new apartment last week," nodded Victoria. "The size of a shoebox, and it's all she can talk about. That and Joe."

"Especially Joe," John agreed.

"And Joe?"

"He's so ecstatic that he barely talks at all," John grinned.

"He deserves it," Victoria said, glancing down at her feet. "When I think how I used to treat him—"

"Rather think how you treat him now," John suggested. "We all regret things we did when we were younger. Joe knows that as well as you do."

Victoria nodded.

"How is Todd?" John asked.

"Could be better," Victoria said. "He's having physical therapy to help get him mobile again, and he's responding reasonably well to his medication, but he was in very bad shape even before being attacked, so it's not going to be quick. Or cheap. We're hoping the fund we set up for him will cover most of his costs. The poor guy's also suffering from withdrawal, but he's sober. Sometimes reluctantly sober, but Nurse Lemmer rules her ward with a rod of iron."

"From what you've told me about Nurse Lemmer, if I were her patient, I think I'd be reluctantly sober too."

Victoria laughed.

"I'd trust her with my life though."

"What will happen to Todd when he is finally discharged?"

"Not sure yet, but I'm hoping Megan Jenkins will be able to offer him work maintaining her property and grounds. She suggested it a while back. I saw her last week but didn't want to bring it up at the moment. She looked so tired and thin."

John nodded.

"Yes, with Maurice in jail and then the divorce proceedings, she's taking strain."

"She needs a break."

"She's getting one. Didn't she tell you? She and Gavin are heading off to Paris for a holiday."

"Paris?" Victoria blinked, before adding ironically, "naturally, that's always my first option when I'm stressed too."

"Naturally," John grinned. "Where else? Maybe you should pay France a quick visit once you're no longer needed at the police station."

"I've actually been offered Steve's position with the police here — if I want it," she said slowly.

"Are you going to stay? It's a big decision to make."

Victoria smiled without answering and carefully opened the box of ashes she held in her hands.

"My mother used to bring us here when we were little," she said, her voice catching a little.

He nodded and placed a hand on her shoulder.

She took a deep breath and scattered the ashes, watching the wind carry them out across the water. She sighed, feeling her shoulders lighten as though she had shaken off the heaviness that had lain across them so long.

She became aware of his hand on her, aware of the unexpected sense of peace it brought, and smiled at him.

"No more nightmares?" he asked, gently drawing her closer.

She shook her head.

"You haven't answered my question yet about whether you're leaving," he reminded her.

She glanced up at him for a moment and slid her arm around his waist. His body felt warm and safe and solid, and she rested her head against his shoulder, at peace at last.

"I just did," she replied.

THE END

Thank you for reading this book.

If you enjoyed it please leave feedback on Amazon or Goodreads, and if there is anything we missed or you have a question about, then please get in touch. We appreciate you choosing our book.

Founded in 2014 in Shoreditch, London, we at Joffe Books pride ourselves on our history of innovative publishing. We were thrilled to be shortlisted for Independent Publisher of the Year at the British Book Awards.

www.joffebooks.com

We're very grateful to eagle-eyed readers who take the time to contact us. Please send any errors you find to corrections@joffebooks.com. We'll get them fixed ASAP.

Printed in Great Britain
by Amazon

87881238R00103